SUN DIAL TIME

SUN DIAL TIME

By DON MARQUIS

Short Story Index Reprint Series

BOOKS FOR LIBRARIES PRESS
FREEPORT, NEW YORK

INTERNATIONAL STANDARD BOOK NUMBER:

0-8369-3676-0

LIBRARY OF CONGRESS CATALOG CARD NUMBER:

79-132119

PRINTED IN THE UNITED STATES OF AMERICA

CONTENTS

AN ANCIENT MARINER

I MET Captain Samuel Billing in the unusual suburb of Hollywood, where incongruities and unrealities jostle one another, and I am not certain to this day whether the soul of a conscious liar or the spirit of a child looks out through the wide, unclouded clarity of his blue eyes. Perhaps both are in his nature.

I had been seeing Captain Billing's beard for many days before I took any note of the captain himself. The beard used to come floating gently out of a canyon at the top of the street where I lived, as if it were a valance of grayish white fog. Sometimes it was accompanied by another beard, sometimes by two other beards, sometimes it was alone. I was spending my winter on the front veranda of a little bungalow, convalescing from an illness, and it was some time before it occurred to my languid mind that these three drifting beards could not, after all, be meteorological phenomena; I made a great effort and concentrated on them, and I was rewarded by the discovery that they were attached to three old men.

But Captain Billing's beard had a quality which was not possessed by its occasional companions. At a glance, it was maritime, or so my fancy told me. I imagined that it had been weathered and seasoned by sun and salt, faded and notched by the winds of the sea.

3

Perhaps an Odyssey slumbered in those harpstrings.

I had been told that there are hermits among the somber surrounding hills into which Hollywood is slashing its way deeper and deeper every year—whether real hermits or fakes, I could never learn; either is credible. But I decided against going up into the gulch to investigate; I might go up there seeking the Arabian Nights and find papier-mâché.

So I followed them one day down toward the city; and I found plenty of papier-mâché in that direction. They went into the enormous stage entrance of Gorman's Babylonian Theater through a wide lane liberally strewn with discarded papier-mâché monsters—broken dragons that had squirmed their last, serpents with battered scales, strange fauna of indeterminate species, and other leftover properties from some spectacular show that had closed.

Animals went in with them, real live animals—camels and dromedaries odorously in the flesh, zebras, elephants, ostriches, giraffes and other exotic birds and beasts, attended by trainers and keepers. The prodigious back door of the building swallowed them all up, and the three gray beards vanished amid the shuffle and the dust.

Almost anything might be going on in Gorman's Babylonian Theater; it is big enough to take care of a political convention, a naval battle and a circus all at the same time. I went around to the front and read a legend over the entrance, in letters as tall as Abraham Lincoln and as brilliant as Bernard Shaw, to the effect

that a great Biblical picture, entitled *The Patriarch,*
with sound and song accompanying the celluloid illu-
sion, was being shown there. I doubt whether Babylon
itself, at the topmost pinnacle of its glory, had anything splendid enough to compete with the façade and
lobby of Gorman's Babylonian Theater. Onyx and
stucco, bronze and authentic marble and imitation marble neighbor one another in bewildering profusion, and
replicas of the ancient idols of vanished peoples rise
again from oblivion, looking faintly sheepish. Probably
the architects and decorators know more about Babylon than I do, but if I knew anything at all about Babylon, I should doubt it.

All about this immense lobby are gilded cages in-
habited by parrots, apes and other jolly chatterboxes,
including the gum-chewing ticket sellers in their own
gilded cage; there is a fountain where little alligators
disport the livelong day; shops where anything from
real diamonds to chocolate sundaes may be acquired
open into the lobby; a continual radio hurls classical
music, religious propaganda and beauty recipes into
this vibrating area, and at night it is ringed as no star
ever was with seven colors of electrical hysteria. To
walk lingeringly through this lobby, yielding oneself
kindly to all its diverse misconceptions, is to put one's
mind into such a condition that nothing one hears or
sees within the auditorium seems too incredible.

The great Biblical moving picture with sound effects,
I found, was preceded by a spectacle, a kind of pageant,
in which the camels, elephants and zebras appeared in

person. My three old men with the beards, garbed in white, rode across the stage on camels, doing their best to look like patriarchs. They had not acted in the film itself; they were just three old men picked up from among the dozens of extras who "peddle the brush" from studio to studio in Hollywood to ride the shambling camels across the stage, and that was all.

But even in this brief appearance the one beard stood out from its fellow beards. It was not a desert beard, and no opulence of suggestive stage effect could make it seem a desert beard. Its roots struck deeper, into more fertile soil; it undulated at the center of a more watery nimbus. Once again I told myself that it must be a seagoing beard—and I still maintain that it was the expression of a seagoing spirit, a soul cradled in the deep, even if the flesh of its owner had never been where the soul had been.

So I lay in ambush for the old man, pounced on him from my veranda, and forced my acquaintance upon him. Within a week he had the habit of stopping every day for a chat and a few doses of the tonic I was taking.

A mild and gentle melancholy pervaded the man. It showed in his speech and manner, and it looked out of his childish blue eyes.

"You're an old sailing master," I suggested one day, early in our acquaintance.

"Yes," he said, "I was in sail." He sighed. "It never done me any good to be in sail." He paused and gathered the end of his beard into his hand and looked at it reproachfully and presently continued: "When you got a mournful fate dogging after you all the time, nothing you are into or nothing you are out of does you any good."

"Your voyages turned out unluckily for you, Captain Billing?"

"So unlucky I don't like to talk about 'em," he said, gazing with pensive eyes as if upon far horizons. "Shipwrecks, and money losses, and personal tragedies of my own of the most peculiar nature, and, on top of that, the terrible ingratitude of four or five gover'ments that oughta been tickled to death for all I done for 'em." He sighed again. "I ain't been bitter," he said. "An old seafarin' man sees too much and goes through too much to let himself get all embittered up by fate; he figgers it's all in the day's work. I ain't been bitter—up till now! But I'm afraid I'm beginnin' to get a little bitter the last few months."

His present grievance, I discovered, was against the movies. This did not surprise me; everyone in Hollywood seems to have his own pet grievance against the movies, and these grievances fall into two general categories—some people cannot seem to get started working for the movies, and others cannot seem to stop.

Captain Billing couldn't get started.

"I can't understand it," he said. "I got the most dramatic story in the world, and I got it all wrote down in black and white, and every word of it's gospel truth, and it all happened to me personal, and they don't seem to realize what a chance I'm givin' to 'em."

For a year he had been sending his story to studio after studio, and it always came back.

"Do you suppose," he said, with a genuinely puzzled look, "that they keep turnin' it down because it's true facts, or because it's too tragic a story for 'em, or because it goes into poetry now and then?"

"Part of it's in verse?" Here was a phase of the cap-tain that I had not guessed.

"Uh-huh," he said, with an affirmative waggle of his beard. "Poetry has always been one of my great admirations, all my life." He added, a little apologeti-cally: "A lot of us old seafarin' men are that way about poetry."

I asked him if I might see it. He looked at me a little doubtfully.

"You're a writer yourself," he suggested; "and of course I wouldn't hint for one minute you'd pick up any of the story knowingly. But it might stick into your mind, and someday you'd be writing something and think of it and not remember where it come from and use it yourself—and that would be some more bad luck for me."

I was astonished at the captain's knowledge that just that sort of thing really does happen sometimes. But he went on:

"Just that very identical thing happened to me one time, with a yarn I told one of you writers—a true story out of my own life, that I'd been aimin' to set down in black and white sometime myself."

But in another week, although I did not mention it

again, he decided that he could trust me and brought me his manuscript, so often rejected by the moving-picture people. It was written with painstaking legibility in purple ink on long sheets of legal-cap paper, and the sheets had been sewn together with coarse black thread.

While I read I reflected on the immense influence moving pictures have had upon the imaginative life of millions of Americans. Near me were evidences of that influence other than the captain's manuscript. Neighboring my bungalow was a Norman tower, built out of stone, and the owner, a retired business man from the Mississippi Valley, habitually sat by one of the windows in his shirt sleeves and sucked oranges. He had seen a tower like that in the films and liked it and had one built for himself. Farther down the block, on the opposite side, were three little bungalows that looked like Egyptian tombs. Their owner had seen some Egyptian tombs in one of Cecil De Mille's pictures and had copied them.

Captain Billing settled himself with a newspaper and pretended to read while I turned the leaves of his script, but he watched me all the time. I present it without editing or alteration of any nature:

CAPTAIN BILLINGS
SCENARIO

Captain Samuel Billing was one of the handyest and smartest sailors that ever commanded one of these old-

fashioned sailing ships, you don't see so many of them
any more, and nobody on the Briny Deep ever saw any
more rough stuff in a thousand ports than Captain Billing, but he remaned a Moral Man.

There should be right at the start a Close-up of Captain Samuel Billing coming out of a Church. It is in
San Francisco, in the early days, and his Pastor comes
onto the Church steps with him. It had ought to be picture that uses dyelog and the Pastor says to Captain
Samuel Billing as follows:

PASTOR—Well, Captain Samuel Billing, you are
about to start on another one of your famous voyages
through the South Seas, and I could wish nothing better than to shake hands with you right here on the
Church steps, right in front of the entire Congre-
gattion, for I know that you will make a tradeing voyge
entirely under the influences of Morality, not like so
many of these wild young sailors, you are a creddit to
this Church.

CAPTAIN BILLING—Well, it would surprise you,
Pastor, what a large quantity of temptations a young
Sea Captain has to resist while making a tradeing
voyge through the Briny Seas, there is wine, women
and song in every port and on everey isleland.

Ha! Ha! said a Voice, he means there are many
Dusky Beauties amongst the islelands, and a handsome
sailor like he might find himself almost ere he knew
it wedded to some isleland Queen.

But there was a sneering tone in the voice and Captain Billing turned and saw the Sneer on the face of his rival, a dark-complexioned young Sea Captain onto whose arm hung the fair blond figure of Miss Nancy Lane with whom both of them had long been in desperate love.

Miss Nancy Lane says to unhand her, please, and she goes on to say as follows:

MISS NANCY LANE—Captain John Morgan, that was a cowardly remark to make, and not the words of a gentleman, you must of been speaking what was in your own black mind.

Her eye flashed fire as she spoke, and the dark Sea Captain sneers directly into Miss Nancy Lane's face.

Then there is a Close-up where Captain Samuel Billing nestles his right hand onto the butt of his Navy revolver, which is hid by the tails of his Prince Albert coat usually, for he will not have Miss Nancy Lane insulted, especially by a rival for her hand, but he thinks better of it after a struggle.

CAPTAIN BILLING—It is well for you, Captain Morgan, that you chose the place for this insult so safely, for you know that I am too much an officer and a gentleman to avenge an insult of this nature right on the Church steps.

Captain Morgan turns pale and goes inside the Church for safe-keeping, his teeth are chattering together, the noise can be made with cocconut shells.

Captain Billing turns to Miss Nancy Lane and goes into poetry as follows:

> That coward has left you in the lurch,
>   Can I see you home, Miss Lane?
> Can I see you home from Church?
>   He ought to be ashamed.

Next there ought to be a Close-up of Miss Nancy Lane smiling at him coyly, and she laughs with gayety and answers him as follows, also going into poetry:

> Oh, yes, Captain Samuel Billing,
>   You can see me safe home from Church,
> I certainly am willing,
>   And glad he left me in the lurch.

> Stroll home with me and meet my Mother,
>   And stay for Sunday Dinner,
> She is setting the table for Another,
>   But you prove to be the Winner.

Captain Samuel Billing and Miss Nancy Lane strolled shyly homeward through long avvenues of el-lum trees, and at first they only talked about the Sermon and the weather. But pretty soon the Close-ups and the dyelog ought to begin to show the awakening into action of love's young dream. She speaks very pleasantly to him of the adventurus life he must of led in

many ports, and he takes her hand and tells her about
some of his adventures, among which is a storm at sea,
and all the perils that he talks about are seen and heard
while he is telling them—you can use your judgment
about music, the sound of waves can be made by rolling buckshot back and forth in a shoe box—what you
want is a swishing noise.

Her Mother is seen waiting in the portico of their
home, standing anxiously with her hand to her forehead, scanning the paths in every direction with tearful
eyes that must of seen better days, and she speaks as
follows:

> Where, O where has my Little Girl gone?
> I never trusted that Captain Morgan.
> She left so innocent this morn,
> To sing in Church and play the organ.

This is the true story of my own life in this scenario
I am mailing to you, and the fact is that Miss Nancy
Lane never did play the organ in church, but she did
sing in the choir and all the other facts are exactly as
set down here in black and white. But if some of the
dyelog goes into poetry it is pretty hard to get away
from the organ, because you have got to get it in that
Mrs. Lane never had any real liking for this Captain
Morgan.

Nancy comes tripping home with the hero of this
picture who she politely interduced to her Mother, and
when they sit down to the fried chicken and hot biscuits

Captain Billing rolls his eyes about the room and remarks as follows:

Well, Mrs. Lane, in glancing around
  I notice that better days have been seen,
Your once costly furniture's somewhat broke down,
  Though what you have left is spic-and-span clean.

Mrs. Lane answers as follows:

MRS. LANE—Well, Captain Billing, it would surprise you how prosperous this family use to be, and
we are still quite arristocratic. I will show you some
trinkets and photographs. Nancy, bring me the Album.
And there are quite a few classy heir looms left, although the real valluable ones I had to pawn, a Mother
must have bread for her child, also a genteel edduca-
tion.

There there is a session with the Album, you can
leave that out if you want to. It really happened, but
it didn't interrest me very much, and maybe it wouldn't
be of much interrest to the movie fans, and finally Mrs.
Lane summons a bright smile through her tears and
says:

My husband sailed the seas a Rover
  I hate to think he has perished.
But now it has been twenty years or over
  Since I said farewell to him I cherished.

This way of making tears with glisserine has got to
be almost a joke these days, so many of the fans are

onto it and laugh about it; they could be made just as easy by holding a little piece of onion in a handkerchief and be a good deal more real and natural, but use your own judgment. Miss Nancy Lane says as follows:

Miss Nancy Lane—I was a Babe in arms when father sailed away on his last voyge. O my poor Father, sometimes I wake up at night screaming and thinking about Sharks and things.

There could be a Close-up run in here of Mrs. Lane holding Little Nancy as quite a young child in her arms, and the little girl is lispping, Oh, Mamma, do you think a Shark got my Pappa?

And her Mother says, Oh, I cannot believe it was a shark, Baby, that would be too cruel a fate, besides he always carried a Testament. No, Baby, something we cannot understand has detaned Pappa from home.

Then a Close-up of waiting through the years.

Well, next you got to get it across some way that Mrs. Lane is kind of kidding the little girl along too. Mrs. Lane has got her own idears all the time and that Testament was just mentioned to make Baby feel happy. His wife was wise that Captain Lane was a good deal more likely to be grabbed off by a girl somewheres than by a shark, it had happened before. From what facts his wife knew about him, he was a pretty bad Egg, maybe she would of forgive him for some of his rough stuff if he had turned up again, and maybe not. But she kept all this from Nancy, she did not want to sullify the girl's purity. And Captain Billing at this time isn't wise to it either. Captain Billing says to Nancy as follows:

> If upon this voyge of mine
>   I should discover your dad
> As a reward of what I would find
>   Would you be willing to wed?

Nancy gives a happy laugh and says it is a bargain, you bet, if you want that in poetry I can mail it in to you later.

But we get a Close-up of Mrs. Lane with her face turned away from the youthful Fond Ones, and by the look onto her face you can tell she is wondering to herself whether it would be such a darn good thing if her husband was to come back, you could show her quite nervously twisting her wedding ring around on her finger, and she steps into the kitchen with some of the dishes off the table and as she puts them absent-minded into the sink she says as follows:

> I wonder should I tell them all,
>   Or keep them still within the dark,
> How often he into sin would fall,
>   Oh, I almost hope he did meet a shark.

But Mrs. Lane makes a great Saccrifice for their sakes, she decides not to tell them, and goes merrily with them down to Captain Samuel Billing's schooner. Captain Billing takes a bucket of paint and paints the name off of his schooner and Christens her the Nancy, you want to be sure and get this in, I spoiled a pare of white-duck pants painting that name, every word in this scenario is gosspel Truth from my own life and adventures.

This was in the old sailing-ship days when I was a young man nearly fifty years ago, the Nancy could show a clean pare of heels to any craft afloat, I will mail into you some newspaper clippings of fast runs she made if you want proof in black and white. Now you got to show the farewells, with some dyelog I will write later, and Captain Billing goes into poetry as follows:

> Bounding over the Briny Deep
>   The Nancy soon will be
> And Miss Nancy Lane on shore will keep
>   Sacred the dimond ring she got from me.

Captain Billing then said he hoped from the profits of this voyage he would come home with sufficient money on him so they could wed and he would pay off the mortgage on Mrs. Lane's home and she could start keeping boarders and he would stay there when he was in port. Right on top of this should be a scene of a big storm cloud at sea, and right across the black cloud are flashes of lightning, and the lines of the lightning flashes had ought to make letters and words spelling out man proposes but God disposes.

CAPTAIN BILLING—Mrs. Lane, if I find Captain Lane I shall bring him back to live in the boarding house too.

Mrs. Lane—Thank you, Captain.

But we see by her face she don't know wether she would want him around or not, probally he would be one of these boarding-house husbands everybody apollogizes for and drunk half the time.

The ship sails quickly into the South Seas and is seen surrounded by islelands and adventures, if it is too expensive to go to the South Seas maybe you could use parts of Cattalena Iseland.

These South Sea islelands is made by Corral insects. It would surprise you how long it takes these insects to make an isleland but they stick to it, there is a great Moral lesson could be brought out here. If real Corral insects under a microscope is too expensive you could use ants with grains of sand in their mouths, and as they worked away there could be a voice going into poetry as follows:

Little bits of Coral,
　　Little grains of sand,
How patient they are and indusstrios and Moral,
　　Making their Native land.

Well, maybe you better leave that out, it is innstructive and riligious, but what the fans like is something with speed to it, and beleive it or not but it takes millions of years to make a good-size iseland, look it up, it would surprise you.

Captain Samuel Billing dives into the South Seas and breaks off lumps of Corral which he makes into a neck-

liss for Miss Nancy Lane. There was more than one
tussle with Sharks but he had his sailor's clasp knife
and they learned here was a man to who they better
give a wide berth.

Next is shown battles with pirates and attacks by
cannabel Nativs and hurricains and navel battles with
Maylays that would come down in ships to rob the
poor Nativs and sell them into Slavery. More than
once they tried to make Captain Billing king of some
isleland for deffending them, but he taught them
against haveing Kings and how to vote and wear clothes
and often he set his foot on iselands no white man
ever discovvered before and hoisted the American flag,
and quelled a Mutiny. You can't go too far in this part
of the picture, this was in the early days, you couldn't
show anything that didn't happen, I was a young man
then and full of pep, you can go as far as you like and
it will all be gosspel Truth. I will write the dyelog for
it later when you decide how far you want to go.

Captain Samuel Billing was approached more than
once with a proposition to marry and settle down by
one of these here isleland Queens, he could of been a
king, and it would surprise you how beautiful some of
those Dusky Beauties are.

You got a great chance here to run in a lot of pictures of Isleland Beauties, you could show Captain Billing teaching them to wear clothes, some break down
and promise to join the Church and wear clothes, some
do not, if it costs too much to send to the islelands for
a lot of Dusky Beauties you can find lots of extra girls

around Hollywood out of work would be willing to tan theirselves up a little and would wear any quantity of clothes or not as you might dessignate, there is a chance here for some nice dances and songs.

Never but once was Captain Billing tempted to wed an Isleland queen, she was a lollapalooza, some queen, some looker. When we think maybe he is about to yeeld his fingers close on the neckliss of Miss Nancy Lane. Close-up. Besides he thinks maybe a lot of stuff might get back to San Francisco, you never can tell, he will be ever faithful to his Nancy.

Well, we got to hurry along now, the big drammatic stuff is all comeing. What I am going to write now is all Gosspel truth, but there's places you've got to use your judgment.

Captain Billing was wrecked on a dessert isleland there was not even a bread fruit tree or other sprig of veggetation or yerbs, all sand and Corral, not even clams and oysters and mussles along the shores, and he was the only one saved from the wreck.

At the same time a few miles away another ship was wrecked by the same storm, and the Captain of it swum to the same dessert isleland, he was the only one saved from his ship.

He is a tall powerful man with bushy eyebrows and a bad record, he is pretty thoroughly tattoed all over, you can see he is an old-timer amongst the South Sea islelands.

Flashes show the hard life he has led as pirate, smug-gler, kidnapper, murderer, gambler, black maler, bigamist, robber, and so forth, as he swims ashore. He is a pretty hard case, this was in the early days, he is wanted for general crime all along the coasts of China and Honnoluloo and Ausstraylia, for years now he has gone by the name of Bully Jackson.

See here, said Bully Jackson, landing onto the dessert isleland, who went and put that American flag up there?

I did, said Captain Samuel Billing, he had swum ashore from the wreck with his ship's flag.

CAPTAIN BULLY JACKSON—Take it down, I hate that flag, once I was an American, but they have made it too hot for me on the high seas.

CAPTAIN BILLING—Touch that flag at your perril.

You work in a good fight here, neither has got any weppons, it is a fist fight. Well, you can't go too far with it, it was a terrible fight, but I was a more sientiffic boxer than Bully Jackson, I knocked him out with the same soaler plexis blow Bob Fisimmons give Corbett, you better take a look at the old films of that fight. Captain Billing now goes into poetry as follows:

The Star-Spangled Banner forever,
    The flag of the brave and the free,
Even here amongst the islelands you shall never
    Put it down on land or sea.

Bully Jackson sits up and sneers but later they are thrown so much together they get quite well acquainted. Misery loves Co. even on a dessert isleland, and they

sit down on the sand and watch for a sail and tell each
other the story of their lives while they are beginning
to starve. You can have the story of their lives flashed
on the screen if you want to but my advice is to leave
it out for we got to speed it up now into the big drammatic stuff.

Hungryer and hungryer they get and no sail in sight.

BULLY JACKSON—Well, sir, have you ever been cast
away before on a dessert isleland, Captain Billing.

CAPTAIN BILLING—Just as often as you have, I
guess, Captain Jackson.

CAPTAIN JACKSON, with a Sneer—I doubt it, young
man.

CAPTAIN BILLING, going into poetry, as follows:

> Although I may seem young in years
>   Long have I sailed the Briny Deep,
> Captain Jackson quit your sneers
>   Or another punch will put you to sleep.

CAPTAIN JACKSON—Keep your shirt on and don't
be trying to pick a row all the time for we both got
trouble enough ahead of us. What I meant was do you
know the invarriable custom that castaways have got
of eating the fattest one to avoid the dangers of starvation. Well, now, Captain Billing, you are the fattest
one of us two. It is one of the invarriable rules of the
sea like women and childern first, but we got no women
and childern here so it looks like you was ellected.

CAPTAIN BILLING, with scorn—Yes, a coward like

you, it goes without saying, would eat women and childern first, if there was any here.

CAPTAIN JACKSON, looking like a hard case, gives a
brutal laugh—Well, it is a rule of the sea that I always lived up to.

CAPTAIN BILLING—I deny that I am the fattest.
Most of this is mussles. You ought to know but if you
don't beleive it I will swing on you again.

CAPTAIN JACKSON—Now, Captain, you keep trying
to pick a quarrel, all I want is this matter settled without trouble according to the invarriabel rules of the sea.

CAPTAIN BILLING's feelings get the best of him and
he goes into poetry again as follows:

No matter how hungry I was for food
  I would pass by the innocent childern
And have more respect for American wommanhood
  Than to prepair it in a caldron.

CAPTAIN JACKSON—mockingly makes a low bow—
I have got to respect your chivvelry, Captain Billing,
but as a matter of fact we are both starving to death,
will you play cards for it?

Bully Jackson has saved a pack of cards from his
wreck, although what Captain Billing saved from his
wreck was the American flag and a Bible, it shows the
two kinds of men they were.

CAPTAIN BILLING—No doubt you are a Card
Sharker but I, too, have a keen eye.

CAPTAIN JACKSON—with another Sneer—Maybe

your keen eye will avale you somewhat, Captain Billing, but pride often goes before a fall.

CAPTAIN BILLING—No doubt you think you are a great card player, but remember that all that glitters is not gold.

So each took a thousand clam shells for poker chips and agreed the one who was cleaned out first was the loser.

Well, now, if I was you I wouldn't show too much of this poker game, maybe a few Close-ups of Bully Jackson cheating and slipping aces and being caught at it, and despare slowly settling deeper and deeper onto his face is enough, but the game really lasted three days. But you got to speed it up, the fans will walk out on you even in these air cooled theaters unless you make it snappy, and the big drammatic stuff is comeing.

Bully Jackson loses his last chip, and we have a Close-up of Bully Jackson with all his wicked past life rushing through his brains, and he says as follows:

> O while the lamp held out to burn
>   I wisht I'd led a better life,
> For now I don't know which way to turn,
>   I'd settle him if I had a knife.

His remorse is something terrible, you could have Close-ups of severil of his wives and families in different ports he is thinking about.

Now here comes a place you got to use your judgment. It is all true I was compelled to go by the invarriabel rule of the sea and make him my viands or else starve and it has been done a million times at sea and nobody ever blamed for it.

But if I was to use my own judgment I would leave out a good many of the detales. I could mail them all in to you if in your judgment you wanted them. But I don't think the fans would like a terrible traggedy like that shown with all the detales and there has been a time or two I kind of hated to think about it myself.

In my judgment it would be a good deal more genteel and refined to skip right from the place where Bully Jackson is shown to be loser to the place where Captain Samuel Billing is sitting on the shore by himself looking out to sea again and you could have him say a little sadly as follows:

CAPTAIN BILLING—Alone on the isleland once more!

If you should want him to go into poetry here again I could mail you a couple of verses. You got to use your judgment, and wether you would want music.

Captain Billing was beginning to get hungry once more when a British gunboat arived, one of these H.B.M.S. ships, Captain John Barker in command, which is cruseing through the islelands for castaways.

They really did that in the old days, every word in this scenario is gospell Truth, sometimes they would pick up hunderds of castaways in a year. Next we see him on board the H.B.M.S. navel vessle in Captain Barker's cabbin and the following dyelog occurs.

CAPTAIN BARKER—Well, Captain Billing, I must

say from the way you been displaying your appetite you must of got quite hungry on that dessert isleland.

CAPTAIN BILLING—It would surprise you, Captain Barker, the demeenor to which an appetite will dessend during starvation.

CAPTAIN BARKER—What, Captain Billing, you don't mean to tell me you got to that unfortunate posittion where us old sailors sometimes find ourselves compelled by necesity to make our companions figure as viands?

CAPTAIN BILLING—Such, indeed, was my unfortunate necesity, Captain Barker.

CAPTAIN BARKER—Well, well, well, Captain Billing, don't take on so hard over it, you couldn't help it, some mighty good people have been compeled to sustain life that way, I guess the King of England himself would of done the same thing if he had of been faced by the same necesity.

And after some more genteel dyelog like that Captain Barker says as follows:

CAPTAIN BARKER—Could you by any chance identtify this man you was compeled to make figure as your viands so I would get a notion who he was? Or do you forget his looks?

CAPTAIN BILLING—His face and appearance will always remane in my memmory.

CAPTAIN BARKER—What markings or detales of apearance did you notice?

CAPTAIN BILLING—It would certainly surprise you, Captain Barker, how tattoed he was.

CAPTAIN BARKER—Do you remember any picture or senttiment tattoed on him that stood out from the rest, have another glass of grog and refresh your memmory, as I have orders to look out for a man of his genneral description.

Captain Billing jogs his memmory with the grog and goes into poetry as follows:

> Of all the beautiful pictures
>   Tattooed on Memmory's wall
> Two turtel doves on his shoulder blades
>   Stands out the clearest of all.

CAPTAIN BARKER—That sounds like Bully Jackson the very man I am in search of now.

BILLING—Yes, he said his name was Captain Jackson.

BARKER—The pirate and murderer and genneral all around criminal.

BILLING—Yes, we got into each other's conffidence before the end came and he told me much of his life.

BARKER—Tell me all you can remember about these turtel doves.

BILLING—Their was one turtel dove onto each shoulder blade and there bils reached out to each other like they was billing and cooing.

Next Captain Barker made a joke you can put in or leave out as you please. When I said they was billing and cooing he said they used to be billing and cooing, but now they was both Billing, meaning my name was Billing. You got to use your judgment, he really said it, and this is a pretty tragic dramma, and it may be the fans would like a little joke now and then, maybe not, I will leave this to you.

CAP. BARKER—Those doves were tattoed there in his young days, so the reports we got on him tell us, before he got to be such a hard case, they represented his fondness for his wife, the legal one, and hers for him.

CAP. BILLING—I guess the man was not all bad.

BARKER—But see here, Billing, I have got great news for you, the turtel doves make the identtity complete, as you sit there you are a rich man.

BILLING—How do you mean, Barker?

BARKER—There was a price on Bully Jackson's head, whoever took him dead or alive is to be rewarded by several governments. Why, man, you got a fortune coming to you.

BILL—I could use money, my ship was not insured, and I owe money for my cargo.

BARK—Look at these figures.

And he jotted down as follows:

PRICES OFFERED FOR BULLY JACKSON DEAD OR ALIVE BY GOVERNMENTS TIRED OF HIS CRIMES

$50,000—Maylay Government, murder and piracy.

$75,000—Chinese govt., robbery, smugling opeium, piracy, kidnapping Nativs.

$100,000—American Govt, murder, perjury, robbery, piracy.

$100,000—English parlament, similar complaints.

$50,000—Ausstralia, genneral crime and miss-
conduct.

$25,000—Philpeen islelands govt., bigamy, mur-
der, arson.

$10,000—By Nativ Cheefs, S.S. Islelands, would
have to be taken in copra, pearl, shell,
etc., not worth claiming.

$410,000, you can scan the figures for yourself.

CAPT. BARKER—resuming dyelog—As you sit there
you are worth nearly half a million dollars, Captain
Billing.

CAPT. BILLING feels like the Count of Monty Carlo,
he gets onto his feet and says—The World is mine!

But Captain Billing all of a sudden gets a sinking
feeling and says:

CAPTAIN BILLING—Is it collectible?

BARKER—Why, what do you mean?

BILLING—I mean I ate up the evidence.

BARKER—Well, you can make out some affadavids,
can't you?

Next we see Captain Samuel Billing in a lawyer's
office drawing up legal papers. But now along comes a
part of this story that ought to be named the Evils of
Red Tape. He showed his affidavids to government
after government and described the markings on Bully
Jackson, but one and all bowed him politely out with
the words as follows:

GOVERNMENT OFFICIALS AND CLERKS—You got to show us more evidence.

Month after month he goes to one government after another but always Red Tape stands in his way and finally he says what is the use of being an honest man and earning all that money by heroic actions and the sweat of your brow if you can't collect any of it? The way these governments have treated him he is allmost ready to turn into an Annarchist.

But one thing holds him back from it and that is the love of a good woman. And then he thinks maybe she will help me figure out some way to prove my story is true and collect my just dues, the old proverb says that love will find a way, I will go home to Nancy. He goes into poetry as follows:

> Over the bounding billows
>   I am sailing home to my Nancy,
> Worth four hunderd thousand dollars
>   But its collection is chancey.
>
> At midnight in my sailor's tent
>   I'm often dreaming of the hour
> When I'll straighten out this predicament
>   And Nancy with wealth endower.

He sails rapidly to San Francisco when this thought strikes him and goes to the home of Nancy and Mrs. Lane there is a joyful greeting, you can put in here all the love scenes you want to, I leave the detales to your judgment.

CAPTAIN BILLING—Nancy, as I stand here I am worth $400,000.

NANCY—looking kind of cute and charming and with a kittenish way—O, goody, goody.

MRS. LANE—O how I have prayed for this happy hour.

CAPTAIN BILLING—But come now dry your tears of joy, and tell me how to figure out some way to collect it.

NANCY—Why, what do you mean?

Captain Billing then tells them the story and requests them sincerely to put the sharpness of a woman's wit to work on his great mental probblem.

MRS. LANE—What were those turtel doves like?

CAPTAIN BILLING—he describes them to her.

MRS. LANE—she turns pallid and staggers.

MRS. LANE—Was there a motto hanging from their beaks with reading matter on it?

CAPTAIN BILLING—Yes, it said that what Providence has joined let no man part asunder, or words to that effect. But tell me, Mrs. Lane, why do you ask, for I feel that all this questioning is leading somewheres.

MRS. LANE—Nancy, get off of that man's lap right away, he consumed your father. This Bully Jackson was really Augustus Lane, he had that motto and those doves tattoed upon our wedding day.

NANCY—getting off his lap—O, O, this is quite a shock to me.

CAPTAIN BILLING—How was I to know it was your father?

MRS. LANE—Yes, that is true Nancy, everybody makes mistakes.

NANCY—It is a matter which I prefer not to discuss farther than to say that the sight of Captain Samuel Billing would always be of the most obnoxious nature to me, even though he were rich as Creesus, which he is not, O my poor father.

She goes and marries Captain Morgan, and Captain Samuel Billing goes out into the world a heart broken man.

"Well," said Captain Billing, laying down his paper, "can you figger it out? Why they won't take it—none of them? Is it the poetry?"

"I think it's the tragedy of it," I replied. "It's too sad."

"Well, then," said Captain Billing, with an air of triumph, "here's a happy ending they could have."

He drew from his inside pocket a smaller sheaf of manuscript and handed it to me.

"In case any of them wrote and said they wanted a happy ending I was going to send 'em that," he said.

I present it.

P.S.—Happy Ending.

In case a Happy Ending is desired, it is easy enough to fix. The true ending of what really happened is what was allready written, but will make changes to suit, what I want is to get some action.

If happy ending is desired, Nancy could be a mere

chit of a girl, say about fifteen years old, and she was born when her Mother was sixteen, and that would make Mrs. Lane 31 years old now, but she don't need to look more than 26 or 27, and is quite beautiful.

She says as follows:

MRS. LANE—I can understand, Nancy, how you could not wish to be associated in matrimoney with Captain Billing, for you were a blood relation to Augustus Lane. But I was no blood relation to him, I never liked him, and the same reasons for scorning Captain Billing do not apply to me, I regard Captain Billing as a hero.

CAPTAIN BILLING—And I prefer a woman of exxperience to a mere chit of a girl who does not know her own mind.

They get married and sail back to the isleland and find a dimond ring which was not consumed which is excepted as proof by all the governments, and that is that, I don't like it so well as what really happened myself, you got to use your own judgment. Or you could make it a gold tooth they find.

I handed the manuscript back to him. I did not like it as well, either. While I was hesitating to say so, a shrill feminine voice cried out near us: "Samuel Billing!"

We had been so engrossed that we had not noticed the approach of the burly woman to whom the voice belonged until she was two thirds of the way up the walk to the veranda.

"You old reprobate! You will run away from me and try to join the movies, will you?"

Here she came onto the veranda and literally took him by the ear.

"Now, Nancy——" said he, in his gently melancholy tones.

"It's taken me three months to find you," she went on, drawing him from the veranda and totally disregarding me. "The idea! At your age! I've a notion to cart you right back to I'way, where you ought to be a-plowin' corn this minute!"

"Now, Nancy——"

But: "Come on!" she said firmly, and jerked Captain Billing out of my life forever, and I still wonder about that beard. Was its maritime quality solely a matter of aspiration, created by the salty spirit of a baffled mariner, or was there some foundation of fact underlying his lively fancy?

THE DOWNEY PEACH

THERE is a bar at Tijuana, Mexico, just over the border, which boasts that it is the longest bar in the world, and that may be true for all I know. Certainly, it is long enough to accommodate many and diverse types of humanity, all the way from magnificent movie actors, taking a day or two off from the arts and ardors of Hollywood, to genuine, full-flavored Mexican gorillas and guerrillas.

Tourists of all grades and categories assemble there to rub elbows—thrillingly—with nondescript gentlemen who live affluently or meanly upon the proceeds of games of skill and games of chance. You may meet up with a professional dope smuggler, or with a deacon of your own home church back in Pennsylvania who is, for once in a way, seeing life (as the Scriptures put it) through a glass darkly. The patrons, in the semiarid years before the repeal of the Eighteenth Amendment, were largely Americans who thought it might do their fallen arches good to slide them back and forth on a brass railing.

It was about the middle of a summer afternoon in 1932, and at about the middle of the bar, that I caught sight of the quizzical blue eye and the hard blue jaw of my friend "Long" Kelley. Kelley, while not so long as the bar itself, amply justifies his nickname. I imagine

37

that very few people have ever been able to reach high enough to give him a good sock on his blue-black jaw; and those who have done so have probably broken their knuckles and wrists doing it. In fact, I can think of only one thing that might be more painful than hitting Kelley solidly; and that is being hit by him. He is as hard as a keg of nails and as sudden as a train wreck.

Kelley had started at the southern extremity of the bar about lunchtime and was genially working his way north. Not having much money of his own, his progress was slow, but, he told me, pleasant. He could count on making a new friendship or reviving an old one about every twenty-five feet, and these kept him going. His friends, new and old, insisted on including him in their invitations; whether because they enjoyed his conversation, or whether because they hoped to put a temporary stop to it, Kelley neither knew nor cared. Conversation is what you get from Kelley. Speech is the greatest need of his existence.

Kelley was accompanied by a young fellow of modest and sorrowful demeanor, whom he introduced to me as George Downey, otherwise known, Kelley said, as the Downey Peach.

"Me and George," explained Kelley, "are living extraneous just now."

"Extraneous?"

"Uh-huh," said Kelley, "like these hoss-doovers on a swell bill of fare. Outside the regular works—extraneous."

Kelley, if he ever had a touch of the Irish brogue,

has lost it. He has, in fact, a conversational style all his own and a vocabulary derived from heaven knows what contacts with life. He is somewhere between forty-five and fifty years old and has seen service in two regular armies and nobody knows how many irregular outfits. His other activities and occupations have been astonishing in their variety. You can't name a place on the face of the earth where he hasn't been. Or, at least, he will say he has been there and tell you a yarn about it. I have known people who told more lies than Kelley, and I have known people who told fewer lies; but I have never known anyone who enjoyed his own tales any more. If he can't find anyone else to listen to him, he will sit down alone, contentedly enough, and talk to himself.

"George, here," said Kelley, with a wink which I was unable to interpret, "is a fightin' man."

Downey blushed at this, gave Kelley a reproachful look and left us. He sat down at a table with a glass of beer and seemed to brood. He was a well-made fellow of middle height, perfectly proportioned and sinewy. His hair was blond and bleached by the sun; he was tanned to the dark ruddiness and streaked tawniness of a peach, and, moreover, there was a kind of innocence about his look that further explained his nickname.

"It hit George where he lived, when I called him a fightin' man," said Kelley. "Poor lad, he's got a secret sorrow. He wanted to get into the big war in 1917, but he didn't, and all these years since he's been melan-

choly about it. I shouldn't have called him that, knowin'
what I know."

He glanced regretfully at the Downey Peach, who
was gloomily absorbing his beer.

"He thinks everybody knows he wasn't in it," said
Kelley, "and it eats him and eats him; and he don't
realize there's a whole world full of people come along
since that scarcely ever thinks of it any more."

"Why didn't he get in, then? Wasn't he old enough?"

"He was eighteen, and he might have made it, but
he was the victim of fate in the form of a nefarious
and unprincipled woman by the name of Myrtle," said
Kelley. "This Myrtle was married to a taxi driver, and
she had a pair of twins, and she eloped with George,
bringin' the twins with her. George, to my mind, was
about as innocent and unworldly as the twins. And this
taxi driver, bein' rid of Myrtle and the twins, elopes in
the other direction and goes to the war, and that's
where George's melancholy and hate for taxis got its
start.

"And before George had been married to her for a
year she has another pair of twins. And all the time
that war was goin' on, poor George was walkin' the
floor nights, with armful after armful of twins, and
workin' hard all day—drivin' the taxi that husband had
left behind—for he had to make a livin' for all them
family responsibilities somehow. And that made him
hate taxis more and more.

"And that war he'd been kept out of was scarcely
more than over, when this Myrtle elopes again. Yes,

and 'twas with another taxi driver, too. If she was going to do that, George figured Myrtle oughta have done it while there was still time for him to get into the war; but this Myrtle was an unscrupulous woman with no regard for George's feelin's, nor for nobody's but her own. And that didn't make George like taxis any better, either.

"George felt Myrtle had disgraced him for life by keepin' him out of that war, so when he is footloose again he starts lookin' around the world for wars to get into, and he's been in most of 'em ever since. He's got to prove to himself he's a warrior, George has. When he isn't in wars, he is always trying to be a box fighter, but his disgrace still keeps eatin' into the poor boy. Nothing can wipe it out for George except another world war and him playin' the leadin' part in it.

"The first time I ever seen George, a referee was countin' ten over him; and George was fightin' the floor because he had a cramp in his wind that wouldn't let him up. And when he finally did get up, he fought his two seconds and the referee and the timekeeper because they told him the bout was over.

"I says to myself, that's a good, willin' lad. So I took the fifty dollars he got for being knocked out that time and become George's manager. The Downey Peach was what I called him, but I never could learn George to box none. He gets so earnest and excited tryin' to abolish the opposition palooka that he lays himself open so wide you could drive a truck through him. And sooner or later a truck always gets drove through him.

He got knocked out so often in the third round that the sports writers quit callin' him the Downey Peach and begun to call him Peach Sundae, and Peaches and Cream, and Canned Peaches, and Peach Cobbler, and names like that which didn't do him any good in his profession.

"And the worst of it was that both me and George knew that he could have licked any one of them fellas that licked him, if only they would quit boxin' for just one minute and fight. For George is a real fightin' man, like I said. He does well in wars, but gloves kinda cramps and smothers his hands, he says.

"We ain't down here fightin' box fights. We're just down here because we are down here. We thought it would be better not to be in the United States for a while. For George got into trouble with another taxi-cab three or four months ago. Me and him was ridin' on a truck, in the outskirts of a city that is quite a ways north and east of here, in behalf of some friends that was in the truckin' business.

"And what was in the truck was some stuff that excited the admiration and envy of some fellas that wasn't friends of these friends of me and George that was in the truckin' business. So one night some fellas that was in a taxi tries to hold up this truck of George's and mine, in the interests of these fellas that wasn't friends of our friends, so as to get the stuff that was in it. And George has the bad luck to bump off the fella that was drivin' the taxi, and there was quite a lot of talk about it, and so we hurried on down here. George says if he had time to think twice, them fellas in the taxi could have had our truck and its contents, and no words bandied, for he ought to realize by this time that taxis is his jinx, in one form or another.

"So, after dinner, if fate decides we're going to have any dinner, we're going to try to get hold of a fella we saw over at Ensenada the other day and make a business connection. Just now, George and me are in the army of the unemployed."

"It's quite a large army these days," I ventured.

"It is," said Kelley, "but it's got some advantages." He ran his hand over his blue-black jaw.

"You don't have to shave every day to belong to that army. I been in armies where, no matter what was goin' on, you had to shave every day. And me, unless I shave *twice* a day, I don't look like I'd shaved once. I was continually explainin' to young officers, half my age and experience, the nature and character of my beard; and finally I got tired of it and quit regular armies for good and all."

He looked up and down the bar, lowered his voice and whispered suddenly:

"George and me is goin' to a war in Mexico, if we can get hold of the money."

"But there isn't any war in Mexico right now," I replied.

"There is so," he said. "Few people know about it. It hasn't been advertised, this war hasn't. It's a private war, and there ain't everybody can get in."

I looked my inquiry, and Kelley proceeded.

"We heard about it over at Ensenada the other day," he said, "from a fella that knows how to get in. This fella has got to go somewhere, because he was too much mixed up with yachts and airplanes."

"What do you mean?" I asked him.

"Well, it's this way," said he: "There's a great big ocean just west of here, and they call it the Pacific, because it's so peaceful. Well, there's a lot of ships comes along here, trustin' to the peacefulness of this ocean, and they ain't anyways wishful of stirrin' up trouble or even notice. All they want to do is to land their cargoes somewheres on the coast of Baja California, and then airplanes picks up the cargoes and takes 'em north over the border to Los Angeles and San Francisco.

"Dope and hootch," I conjectured.

"This fella didn't put a name onto the cargoes, so I couldn't tell you," said Kelley discreetly. "But, anyhow, a lot of busybodies has got on the trail of them fellas, and they're goin' into the interior to join this war, temporary, anyhow. And this fella that George and me is goin' to see this evenin' is takin' quite a bunch of fellas he's picked up at Ensenada and here and there. They're kinda rough fellas, most of them, and they want to get away from where they are at. And so they feel like it would be good policy to be working at something like a war where there is a lot of other fellas around, with guns and things, which is all friends of theirs, in case somebody comes along with papers which they would like to serve.

"So George and I thought we would go and join this

war, too, for a little while, anyhow, till things kind of blows over elsewhere."

Kelley paused, and then added, "If we can get hold of fifty dollars apiece."

"Why fifty dollars?"

"It's like this," explained Kelley: "This is a kind of a pay-as-you-enter war. It costs fifty dollars to get in. But, after you are in, you stay as long as you like, and it don't cost you anything more, and when anybody comes to inquire about you, why, they don't get you. And there's a lot of fellas which that is worth fifty dollars to right now, till better times comes in certain lines of business and things here and there blows over. And anyway, as George says, it's a war."

I earnestly requested more information about this peculiar and, in a way, secret war.

2

"Did you ever hear of the Yaqui Indians?" said Kelley. "I don't know much about 'em myself, except from hearsay. But, from what I hear, the Yaqui is quite an Indian.

"The Yaqui, in his peaceful moments, is a kind of an Egyptian mummy that ain't been embalmed yet. And he sets down contented on a rock and makes baskets and pottery, and eats beans and thinks about the times, hundreds of years ago, when them Mexican pyramids was built. He gets himself into all these guidebooks and tourist folders about Mexico, and kind words is said about him by lady lecturers from colleges in the East, who figure out he is all cultured up and artistic in his own way and probably pretty much oppressed.

"But when he ain't peaceful, he ain't. When he gets irritated by something and goes on the war path, he's bad. And he can go to war more economical than anything except a cactus plant or a scorpion. He's used to livin' on nothin' but sand and gravel, and he don't need any more water than an Arizona bullfrog, which sometimes reaches the age of five years before it learns how to swim.

"It seems two or three hundred miles south and east of here is an American rancher by the name of Simms, who owns more acreage than anybody in the world except the British Empire, and his kingdom is bordered on one side by a range of desert mountains which is as full of Yaquis as an anthill is of red ants. Simms is an oldish man and has been there all his life, and he never had any trouble with any kind of Mexican except these Yaqui Indians I'm telling you of. About two years ago they come down out of the hills and kidnaped part of his family—his wife, one of his daughters, and his two boys. They sent word that unless he paid ransom he'd never get 'em back.

"Simms sent 'em word that he'd see 'em all in hell before he paid a dollar, and the war started. It's been goin' on two years now, and he's got one of his sons back, but they're still holding the other one and his wife and daughter.

"The Mexican government is neutral, to a certain

extent. They don't want to start any noisy operations, for fear it would get into the papers that another revolution had broke out in Mexico and scare off tourists and possible investors in oil and minerals. They got a troop of cavalry stationed near there to act as a kind of umpire. They've sent word to the Yaquis that if the captives are harmed, they'll send an army and clean 'em up, all of 'em, forever. And, on the other hand, they won't let Simms bomb the Yaqui hills from airplanes, or anything like that, for fear that would attract so much attention outside it would get into the American papers.

"Simms, him and his cowboys, fought it for two years, with what men they could pick up and pay. But now Simms is busted with the expense. He furnishes you with a horse, if you join him, and he boards you, and he's been gettin' in a lot of this class of fellas that is wanted other places. But you got to bring fifty dollars' worth of ammunition with you, or else that much money, for the privilege of stringin' along with Simms and his army."

Kelley paused and looked thoughtful.

"There's where me and George is aimin' to go," he finally said, "but we ain't got the fifty dollars."

"And no prospects?"

"George," he returned, "is an innocent kind of a fella, and I noticed often that kind is luckier than others at roulette. If I had as much as ten dollars, I'd send George to the tables. Who knows? You never can tell!"

I wondered if the whole tale had been a preamble to this touch. But I lent Kelley the ten dollars. . . .

It was almost exactly a year later that I met him again, at the same place. George was not with him. I asked for George.

3

George (said Kelley) is now the prosperous half owner of one of the largest ranches in the known world, happily married, and, by this time, for all I know, walkin' some more twins through the small hours of the night.

Before we go any further, I want to ask you if George ever sent you the ten dollars he borrowed the last time I seen you? No? Well, that ain't like George, and I can't understand it. I give him the permanent New York address you give me that day, and George is well able to pay his debts. I'll write him and remind him myself.

I sent George to the roulette table, and he was lucky. I won't go into the ups and downs of it, nor the agonizin' suspense when it dwindled down to the sum of $1.50, nor the joy and uplift when it started gradually up again. But I dragged George away from the table when it reached the sum of $167.50. He wanted to stay on, and of course he woulda lost every cent of it and not now be half owner of the biggest cattle ranch in the world. He owes that to me, George does, but he's one of them innocent fellas that don't know what they owe to other people, and consequently seldom pays it.

We didn't need but $100, so we spent the $67.50 on drinks before we left Tijuana that night.

There was kind of a bad omen come and perched onto George before we got really started. When we left a place, where we had been spending some money for drinks, to go to another place to spend some more money for drinks, we went in a taxicab which had a San Diego license plate onto it. And George gets into an argument with the driver, who says his name is Smith, and Smith hits George with the thing he uses to crank the car with and lays him out and gets away with his taxi. And it seems this Smith had had trouble in San Diego, which was why he had left there and was huntin' a quiet little war or somethin' in Mexico himself; which he told us before him and George declared war onto each other. And George and me met up with our Ensenada friend, and we was plumb into the middle of that Yaqui war before the lump on George's eye had turned from blue to yellow, and George hating taxis more than ever.

Me and George seen right away, when we got to old man Simms' ranch, that this war was different from any war either one of us had ever been at before, and the reason why it had lasted so long without ever getting anywheres in particular with itself. It was a war where a big valley was fightin' the mountains, so to speak, and neither one of 'em could get at the other one in the right way to do much damage.

Old man Simms' ranch took in the whole extent of

a high valley, and the Yaqui country was a kind of a big semicircle of hills around the north and west of him. Canyons and gorges come down out of the hills and opened out into his plain. And out of them would come bands of Yaquis, bent on such devilment as stealin' cattle and goats and pickin' off careless cow hands and Simms-ites that got too far away from the main bunch. But there was long open stretches between the hills and the ranch houses, and no considerable gang of Yaquis could cross them plains, in an effort to destroy the main works, without bein' seen miles away and prepared for.

On the other hand, Simms and his roughnecks couldn't get very far into the hills. The mountains is all cut up with these here canyons and ravines and gulches and passes that twists in and out, every which way, with a thousand places where fifty men could stop five hundred. So the fightin' had been a kind of a stand-off, mostly takin' place in the neighborhood of the foothills, where the mountains broke down into the plateau.

The thing that made old man Simms the maddest was that these Indians, every now and then, would actually get away with a bunch of his cows and drive 'em off into the upcountry.

"There's some traitorous white man joined them Injuns recently," he says to me, a few days after we joined. "Or, at least, somebody who is able to write the English language. Look at the note I got day before yesterday!"

Simms was one of them men you meet in the South-west which you can't tell how old they are by fifteen years on account of them being so weathered. He was as spry as a kid, but he was dried and burned till his face looked like a piece of brownish, dried-out cactus stem in a double-handful of snow, which snow was his white hair and beard, which he had been neglectin' till it was drifted in every direction and blowed and shifted when the wind blew. And he had a pair of gray eyes that looked like little lumps of ice in the midst of that.

"Lookit this here insult, Mr Kelley!" he says. And handed me a piece of paper tore out of an address book and wrote on with a lead pencil, with ignorant kind of handwriting. I saved it; I got it here with me now. Read it:

Dere Mister Simms, Pardon us for taking the calfs, as we don't ordinary fancy your cattel till they gets beef critter size, but Missis Simms and yure Dotter says they would like veele, so we gets some veel for them, and they sens word they is well and happy as could be expected, but would now like to go home, and wish you was not so stubborn about paying ransim; and they are a great expense to us, so you better change your mind and pay ransim.

(Signed) OLD MAN YAQUI.

Simms, he snorted when he showed it to me. "Old Man Yaqui!" he says to me. "Old Man Yaqui!" he says. "No Injun ever wrote that, nor called himself

that—it ain't in the least like 'em! Mrs Simms wants
veal! Why, Mr Kelley, she never cared a whoop for
veal, nor my daughter Dolores, neither! That's some
renegade white man, I tell you, that's joined them
yaller thieves! Day before yesterday I come onto the
dead body of Tom Hastings, one of my best vaqueros,
up in the foothills—he'd gone to gather up stray calves,
and they'd got him from ambush, and took his calves
and pinned this note to his shirt!

"By Gad," he says, "I'm goin' up there—I'm goin'
up there myself, if it's for no other purpose than to
wring the neck of the fella that wrote this note! Mrs
Simms wants veal, does she! I'll take somethin' besides veal up there for them Injuns to chew on! Fifteen
head of calves and another good cow hand gone!"

He was on a horse, in front of his ranch house, and
the horse pranced and danced on its hind legs, as if it
was as mad as he was, when he turned and shook his
fist at the line of mountains, all saw-toothed and purple
in the distance.

"I'm gonna get me airplanes!" shouts the old man,
still shakin' his fist, while twenty or thirty of his roughnecks gathered round to hear him orate. "I'm gonna
get me airplanes and comb them hills with bombs till
they ain't a single Injun left alive, nor even a rattlesnake! And if the Mex government don't like it, I'll
sail them airplanes down to Mexico City and bomb
their capital! I'm gettin' mad at this war, I am! Mrs
Simms wants veal! The impidence of that insult! The
hell she wants veal! I bet she never said a word about

veal! By gosh, I'll veal 'em! When I get ahold of the treacherous white man that wrote that note, I'll wrap him in a bale of barbwire with a layer of cactus next his hide and roll him down a mountain! Veal! Mrs Simms wants veal!"

And with that he would of toppled off his horse, but his ranch foreman, Bob Herbert, caught him and eased him to the ground.

"Uncle Abner," says Herbert, mildlike, "you don't want to be gettin' so mad like that, or you'll bust another blood vessel in your brain. Come into the house with me and I'll fix you one of them milk punches you like." And he helped him in.

"What does he mean," I asked a fella all decorated up with guns and general war tools who was standin' near, "by *another* blood vessel?"

"We figure," said this fella, "that Uncle Abner has busted seven or eight blood vessels that way the last three months. He can't get so he takes this war easy, as a matter of course, in spite of how long it's been going on. There was a young doctor down here from San Diego a few months ago who helped him through the first one of these spells, and he figgered Uncle Abner had busted a blood vessel that time, and I counted six more blood vessels since then myself. One trouble with Uncle Abner is, he's kinda lost his sense of humor about this war."

This fella, whose name was Cummins, comes a step nearer to me and says, confidential-like, "In spite of what Uncle Abner says, I ain't got any doubts what-

ever that Mrs Simms asked for veal and raised so much
hell about it that the easiest way out for them Injuns
was to come down and get the veal. It would be like
Mrs Simms to raise hell till she gets what she wants.
She always did."

"She sounds like a peppy old lady," I says.

"She ain't old," says Cummins. "She ain't more 'n
thirty-five at the most. She's his second wife. She's
always put in her whole time raisin' hell till she got
what she wanted."

Well, it was the very next afternoon that Mr Simms
—or Uncle Abner, as they all called him—busted another blood vessel. He was a grand old man, Uncle
Abner was, and he must of been as full of extra blood
vessels as a shad is of little bones. After he had one of
those bustin' spells he'd drink another milk punch and
seem all right again. But a man of his age can't go on
bustin' blood vessels like that without it having some
effect on his general health in the long run, neither.
Bustin' all them blood vessels would result in a nervous
breakdown, if it wasn't stopped. The next afternoon
Uncle Abner took me and George and about twenty
more fellas and went on a scoutin' expedition over
towards the mountains, where there was a crick come
down a canyon out of the hills. He wanted to see about
puttin' a wire fence acrost the arroyo, so his cows
wouldn't stray too far up where they could be am-
bushed.

Our party was ridin' up the canyon, the horses pickin'
their way among the stones in the crick bed and on the

banks, when something come rattlin' down the canyon with a racket like Fourth of July in hell and made right for us. It was calculated to bust anybody's blood vessels. It was a kind of an armored car, and it was snarlin' like a mountain lion and spittin' machine-gun bullets. I ain't any mountain climber, but it seems my horse was, and he went up the side of that arroyo among the boulders like an airplane pantin' for altitude. He shed me off behind a boulder and I laid there, and he went on up, and I never seen him since. Down below, this thing was still yowlin' and snortin' bullets, but it couldn't follow us uphill, and pretty soon I realized that two other men was behind my rock. One of 'em raised up and started firin' a six-gun down at that car.

"She wants veal, does she?" I heard him say. "I'll veal her, all right!"

It was Uncle Abner, and right after that he laid back on the gravel, and whether it was his blood vessels I heard poppin', or only guns, I don't know.

The other fella back of my rock was George Downey. George was lyin' on his stomach, workin' a rifle for all he was worth, and he didn't look pretty, because a machine-gun bullet had creased his forehead, and the blood was all over his face. He was madder 'n I ever seen him.

"Kelley, do you know what that thing is?" says George, shakin' the blood out of his eyebrows.

"What?" I asks him.

"It's a taxicab," says George. "I come down here to get away from 'em, and they come down here after me, chasin' me! Yes, and did you see who was drivin' it? Huh? It's that fella Smith, who hit me over the eye! He's come down here and joined the Injun side of this war against the whites—which is just what a taxi driver would do!"

"Always wantin' somethin', that woman!" says Uncle Abner, bustin' blood vessels and workin' his gun. "Veal! Veal!"

"Taxicabs," says George, "is my jinx! But someday the worm will turn!"

All around us, from behind rocks and boulders, the Simms-ites was pourin' down a hot fire on that taxicab. They had took it and riveted plates of iron all over it, and you could hear our bullets going *Wham! Wham!* when they hit it. Pretty soon things got too hot for it, and the machine turned around clumsy-like down there and lumbered and jolted back up the trail into the hills again.

We got old Uncle Abner back to the ranch house about dusk, and lubricated his arteries with some milk punches, and held a council of war.

It was then that George Downey showed he had the makin's of a general.

"Uncle Abner," he says, "horses will never get us anywhere in this war—you lost three of them this afternoon, besides a couple of men that musta been nearly as valuable. We got to go up through them passes with armored trucks and dynamite and blast our way to wherever they're holding your family. For somewheres up there is a stronghold where they've got 'em hid out, you take my word for it. We got to inter-duce some strategy into this war. We'll go in from a dozen ways at the same time, and hold all the trails, and work towards the center——"

"There ain't any center to them hills," says Uncle Abner. "But the trucks and dynamite is a good idea. We'll start gettin' the trucks ready in the mornin'."

The next mornin', whilst all hands was workin' on the trucks, up to the ranch house comes a couple of scouts with a Yaqui Indian. He had come down out of the hills with a white flag, and he had a message for old man Simms.

"Read it to me, Mr Kelley," says Uncle Abner to me. "I left my specs up in that arroyo yesterday."

It was wrote on a leaf of the same notebook as had been used to convey the insult about the veal to Uncle Abner. I saved it. Here it is:

Dear Abner:

Why have you always been so stingy ever since I married you? Simply because I am your second wife? I should think you would at least have some considera-tion for your daughter, Dolores, and your son, Jerry, even if you don't care what happens to me. Quit being so stubborn and stingy, and send the ransom money right away. I am tired of it here, and I have set my heart on seeing that Century of Progress Exposition at Chicago. And I need some clothes. Now get busy, old Skinflint, and raise the money.

YOUR LOVING WIFE.

"Raise the money!" yelled old Uncle Abner, tearing out handfuls of white whisker in his rage and trying to throw them towards the mountains. "Raise the money! She thinks I'm a bank! She thinks I'm a mint! She oughta know I'm busted! She does know it, and she don't care! She never did care! I got no money left! In another six months I'll have no cows left! I've got nothin' left but land, and what the hell good is land! Here, Herbert! Bob Herbert! Shake me up a milk punch, quick!"

"Yes, Uncle Abner," says Herbert.

"No! Don't shake up that milk punch!" yells Uncle Abner. "Write to that San Diego life insurance agent —you know his name. Tell him to cash in all them policies and hold the money for me! I'm gonna bust my last artery and die, and not a cent of life insurance will that woman get, not a cent! Chicago fair be hanged! I'll take a fair up into them mountains that 'll shake the world down! Got to go to a fair, has she? I'll go up there with fire and dynamite and bust my last artery right in that woman's face! That's what I'll do! Hurry up with that milk punch!"

"I thought you said you didn't want it," says Herbert.

"You gimme what you know I need," says Uncle Abner. "Do you want me to get a nervous breakdown with these blood vessels? You gimme my medicine, and then all of you get outa here and go to work on them trucks. She wants a world's fair, does she? I'll take her a world's fair on wheels! Stingy, am I? I'll spend all her life insurance policies on dynamite and show her whether I'm stingy or not!"

A coupla days after that, when we were gettin' our trucks fixed up, along comes that Mexican captain who was in charge of the cavalry, and says he doubts whether the government will approve of dynamite tactics against the Yaquis; and Uncle Abner better wait till he sends for orders and gets word.

"You go down to Mexico City and tell your government it can't stop me," says Uncle Abner. "Listen, now —I've played the game square with your government so far. I ain't got international, have I? Well, if your government makes a single move to stop me, I'm gonna get international! I'm gonna send for newspaper reporters and press agents and spread this war over every paper in the known world. And how's Mexico City goin' to like that?"

4

So the government says nothin', and into the hills we go, by different trails and passes, eleven trucks of us, with war tools and dynamite bombs till you couldn't rest, and that was the grandest mountain warfare ever since Napoleon Bonaparte and Julius Caesar and Hannibal the Cannibal climbed to the top of the Alps and slid down into Italy on the seat of their britches, with fire in their eyes and the shout of "E pluribus unum" on their lips.

But, as Uncle Abner said, there wasn't no center to

that country to converge on. In the second place, them
trails wasn't built for trucks; they wasn't even built for
wide-footed horses; some of 'em wasn't even wide
enough for burros. Not that a Yaqui cares. He goes
afoot, and he can go upside down like a fly or a spider
on the ceilin' if he's in a hurry to get somewheres and
the land lays that way, which it mostly does. We went
sluggin' along, where the trucks could go, and then we
went on horses and burros till *they* couldn't go no further, and then we went on foot and sometimes on hands
and knees.

We'd anchor a truck in a pass and work outwards
from it; and where you expected to run onto a gang of
them Indians, there wasn't none. And where you
thought there wasn't none, all of a sudden there would
be a couple of hundred, and you'd know they was there
because they would be rollin' boulders downhill onto
you and splatterin' bullets all around you and through
you, and when you got to where you thought they was
at, and devastated the vicinity with dynamite grenades,
there wouldn't be nothing there at all except a land-
slide comin' straight at you, which you had shook loose
yourself. We made more racket up in that country,
what with echoes and avalanches, than any war I ever
been at except the big noise in France.

You oughta seen Uncle Abner dancin' on a summit
like a mountain goat, with bullets and rocks combin' his
long white whiskers, slingin' sticks of dynamite into a
ravine, his arteries poppin' with rage and excitement,
like a burst of machine-gun fire, and the vultures of the

hills turnin' faint in the air above his head from the sulphurous profanity that emitted itself out of his aged lips. I never seen a nice old man have such a happy time in my life.

We may have slew millions of Yaquis, and I don't see how we could help slayin' somethin' up there, all the fuss we made. But the truth is, I never yet seen a dead Yaqui and few live ones. But for three weeks we shook them mountains from toenails to tonsils, and then one afternoon I passed out of the hullabaloo sudden. From somewheres or other, up a mountain pass, comes that armored taxicab again, with an incompetent Injun drivin' it, and it passes by my vision with a lurch like a drunken elephant and up the rough slope. And then comes George, chasin' it, standin' up in a truck, heavin' grenades at it. Just as the taxi reached the summit of the pass there was a hell-roaring burst of flame and noise, and then all the mountains in the world fell on top of me. And, as the sayin' is, I knew no more.

It was about ten days later I come to myself in a hammock on the veranda of the ranch house. Uncle Abner, with most of his hair and whiskers gone, and bandages all around his head, was settin' in a chair drinkin' a milk punch through a straw.

"How's your war, Uncle Abner?" I says, to pass the time of day.

"Still goin' on," says Uncle Abner. He jerked his head in the direction of the mountains. And then Abner drops his milk punch and gets to his feet.

"By gravy!" he says. "Feel that!"

He staggered where he stood, and I felt the hammock I was in begin to swing. And then, in another minute, we heard the noise of cattle, bellowin' and racin', and a bunch rushes right by the ranch house, runnin' drunk and staggery; and the ranch house seemed to kind o' twist and heave.

"Look," says he, "look!"

I looked west, where he pointed, and that range of mountains was twistin' like a snake; and there comes a dull roar from over there in the west. The sun was gettin' ready to go down, gold and red, behind the purple ridge, and the purple twisted itself into the gold of the sky. It was an earthquake—the same one that shook up Los Angeles and Long Beach. Yes, sir! I figure George started that earthquake goin' up the coast, with all his blastin' down there—he started them landslides, and they ran north. That was George's personal earthquake!

And while we looked, totterin' and staggerin' on our feet, out of the west, with the purple and gold behind him, comes George himself, at the head of a parade, like a conquerin' king of Babylon returnin' in triumph from the wars! In a truck he was, drivin' it himself with one hand, and his other arm was around a girl. Eight trucks was bouncin' after 'em, all that was left of our eleven, and bouncin' is right! For the ground itself was heavin' in billows like the waves of the sea, and them mountains in the distance was bumpin' their foreheads together, and the gold and purple was jumbled in the heavens, and the men in the trucks was yellin', and the ground was shoutin' and roarin' with 'em.

George leads his parade across the rockin' earth up to the veranda.

"Here's your daughter, Uncle Abner," he says. "Me and her is goin' to get married. . . ."

5

Kelley paused from his narrative and refreshed himself with a long draft of ale.

"But Mrs Simms?" I asked him.

"He hadn't brought her," said Kelley. "The daughter he had brought, and the son he had rescued, but not the wife."

"But——"I began.

"Uh-huh," said Kelley. "I asked him why. Uncle Abner didn't, though. And I figure Uncle Abner gave him half the ranch by way of double reward—part for rescuin' his children, and part for not rescuin' the wife."

"It does seem a little hard on the lady," I demurred.

"So I said to George," replied Kelley. "And George says, 'Oh, I dunno, Kelley! Leave her lay! Let her and them Injuns and that Smith fight it out. If I had brought her along, things woulda been liable to get kinda complicated. You know who this Mrs Simms is, Kelley? She's that Myrtle I was married to once't.'"

RATTLESNAKE GOLF

MAJOR STACEY eased his long, lank frame into a wicker chair next mine on the hotel veranda, rolled himself a cigarette, borrowed a match and inquired:

"Well, how did you like our sun-kissed California Christmas?"

It was my first winter in Hollywood, and I was discovering that natives and old residents like to hear newcomers enthuse over the wonderful climate from time to time; so I did the proper thing.

"But," I added, "you don't look so cheerful yourself, Major."

"I'm not," he returned. "A couple more Yuletide seasons like this last one, and I'll be on a downtown corner with a tin cup making indigent noises. Santa Claus took more toys away from me than he left in my stocking this year."

"What's been the trouble?"

The Major blew a couple of meditative smoke rings and appeared to consider profoundly. "I impute my financial downfall," he said finally, "to golf and unwise supersalesmanship—to that and the notions of Colonel Elwood B. Sanford."

"You mean the gentleman with the long, white hair and the broad hat who comes here to see you sometimes?"

"Uh-huh, that's the Colonel. He tries to make up as he thinks a Southern colonel of the old school ought to look. But he isn't one. I've heard him try to put it across on innocent Easterners like yourself that he's an old Californian, but he isn't that, either. My private opinion is that he spent the greater part of his life touring the Middle West as an old herb doctor in a medicine show."

A sudden involuntary contraction of the Major's facial muscles mangled his cigarette, and it was with a hard look in his eye that he added: "He's got a past, Colonel Elwood B. Sanford has. And if he played the deceitful part I think maybe he played, he's got more past than he's got future."

"Tell me about it," I invited. During our six weeks' acquaintance Major Stacey has learned to value me as an auditor, because I know nothing whatever about the West and cannot be sure when he is exaggerating. Indeed, I cannot even be sure when he is departing entirely from the realm of possibilities just for the sake of indulging his own sense of humor and astonishing me.

Another reason the Major cultivates my society is the hope that he will someday sell me something. I find him an interesting raconteur, but—not to cast suspicion upon a man who frequently and fervently affirms his own business integrity—I don't think I shall ever have the impulse to invest in any enterprise which he recommends.

"I've known Colonel Elwood B. Sanford," began Major Stacey, "about five years; ever since he first showed himself in this town. And, until the events of the last week transpired, I've rather admired the man; admired him for his salesmanship ability and for his enthusiasm. He's a genius; sometimes he goes too far, but the genius is there. He isn't always sound, he hasn't always got judgment, but he's got brilliance.

"When he's going good, he could sell roller skates to an old ladies' home. For a while I employed him in my own real estate business, first giving him a careful warning, of course, never to misrepresent anything. I don't know whether he heeded it or not, but I've got my suspicions. I've got a reputation to maintain in this great and growing metropolis, and I've never yet made a statement nor put over a deal that wouldn't bear scrutiny. I've told you a lot of yarns about the West and my experiences, and did you ever catch me once in the slightest deviation from gospel truth? No, sir, not once!

"After about a year, the Colonel left me and started his own real estate office; but there's one thing we've always had a sort of partnership agreement about. That's my little place back in the hills, by Cactus Canyon. I'd told him that if he could sell that place for me, I'd give him an enormous commission—he could have fifty per cent of the entire proceeds for his own.

"You see, it's not been so easy to sell. He's tried several times, and so have I, and I'm a pretty fair salesman myself, of the old-fashioned, conservative type. I could never understand why that little place should be so hard to get rid of; for it's got everything in the way of diversities and opportunities that heart could wish. It's only about forty miles from here, and it's my belief that someday this metropolis will grow right up to its edges and spill into it.

"About two weeks ago the Colonel—and I don't really believe that old fourflusher is any more a real colonel than I am a major—came over here to see me, and he sat down in that very chair you're in now, and he says, with his voice all husked up with excitement:

" 'Major, I've got a sucker!'

" 'What do you mean, Colonel Sanford?' I asked. 'I don't understand you.'

"I never like to have slang expressions like that addressed to me, especially right out on a hotel veranda with people coming and going. It cheapens legitimate commerce, and it doesn't inspire confidence if it should be overheard.

" 'I mean a boob,' he says. 'A hick. A customer.'

" 'Colonel,' I says, 'are you speaking of a business prospect?'

" 'Uh-huh,' says he, 'a fall guy. And this sap and that Cactus Canyon stuff of yours were just simply made for each other. He's a retired banker who's got interested in the West. And he's some kind of a New Yorker, or else maybe an Englishman—I can't make out which. Maybe both.'

" 'How do you know he is?' I said.

" 'He looks like it to me, and he talks like it, and he leaves his fork in his left hand like it.'

" 'I don't savvy,' I says.

" 'You know what I mean,' says the Colonel. 'He cuts up his grub with his right hand, and then doesn't lay down his knife and change his fork. Keeps the fork in his left and eats that way.'

" 'Say,' I said, 'that's a pretty foxy stunt, too. It leaves the knife in the right hand in case trouble starts anywhere near. I guess they have to do that in those Eastern towns nowadays on account of so many gunmen and bandits coming into the night clubs and restaurants all the time. Every time I see a newspaper I'm glad I live in the West, where one of these Chicago or New York bad men I read about can't get me. But how do you know he's a banker?'

" 'He's living at my hotel,' said the Colonel, 'and I heard a new arrival who was an acquaintance of his ask him if he was having a little vacation from the banking business. We'll take him out into the great open spaces.'

" 'Isn't there any way,' I asked, 'to sell him that land without letting him see it? That's where we have always made our mistake before; we went and showed it to people.'

" 'Listen,' he says, 'I've got the psychology of this superselling campaign all figured out. The rougher the country, the better. This fellow is sold on the romance and color and picturesqueness of the West. We've got to mingle all that in with our business talk in just the right way. He's all hopped up right now with the idea of going out with one of the scouts of the old Indian days.'

" 'You mean the old Indiana days, don't you, when you were selling electric belts at the county fairs?' I asked him.

" 'Well, I sold 'em, didn't I?' says the Colonel. 'I've got this thing all fixed. The day before we go out, I'm going to send out a couple of these Hollywood moving-picture cowboys, and———'

" 'What for?' I interrupted him. 'If he wants to see cow hands, he can see some of old man Thompson's genuine ones. There's always three or four driving the flivver around to listen to the radio in my shack when I'm up there.'

" 'No,' said the Colonel, 'they won't do. They won't look like the cowboys he's seen on the stage and the screen—won't talk like it or act like it or dress like it or be fooling around with guns all the time. They haven't got the picturesqueness of those camera-wise boys. All they understand is how to handle cattle. And, say, you'd better make sure there are some cows standing about, where this prospect can see my movie boys herding them, or rounding them up, or whatever it is that cowboys do.'

"The Colonel isn't really much less ignorant about the real West than you are; he's lived in hotels and boarding houses ever since he's been out here.

" 'Cows?' I said to him. 'There's no cows on my place.'

" 'Well, why don't you have cows on it?' he says, sort of peevish.

" 'If you were a cow,' I said, 'you'd get so, yourself, you'd want something to eat besides rattlesnakes and golf balls.'

" 'Golf balls?'

" 'Uh-huh. Since you were up there last I've fixed up a golf course of my own. There must be five or six hundred golf balls lying around there now in places they can't be played out of.'

" 'Say,' says he, 'that's great. This gets better and better. This fellow told me yesterday all the courses he'd seen around Hollywood were too flat to suit him. Why, some of the biggest deals in the business world are pulled off on golf courses these days! It's a system. You let the prospect beat you, and while he's still feeling tickled about it you get his name on the dotted line. And I'm quite a golfer myself. What's par on this course of yours?'

" 'On my golf course,' I said, 'it's not so much a question of what you can go round in. The question is: Can you go round? It's a little rough here and there.'

" 'Fine!' said the Colonel. 'He'll love that. And he'll be amused at the idea of a golf course being mixed up with this old romantic West we're going to show him. You go up ahead of everybody, with supplies to last a week or so, and borrow some of old man Thompson's cows to make the place look right.'

"I agreed, but I doubted whether Thompson would lend me any of his cows. One of the reasons he has to have hired hands is to keep his cows off that little place of mine. Thompson's ranch is over beyond the hills from me, and it's about the size of New England or Germany, with plenty of feed and water on it; and since the price of beef had been up the last couple of years, he naturally doesn't want to lose any more cows than he has to. And every time any of his cattle get onto my place they seem to strike bad luck, somehow. Sand-storms bury 'em. Or boulders roll down and hit 'em. Or insects and things sting 'em till they swell up and burst. Or they fall into canyons and die of thirst. Or else animals molest 'em.

"One of the most surprising things to me is the amount of animal life that place supports as compared to the vegetation. The only way I can figure it out is that the animals make their living by eating each other. That place just gave its heart and mind and soul to cactus when the world was made. Enemies of mine have tried to spread the story that it's the only land in the world that isn't fertile enough to grow sagebrush. But the truth is that with all that cactus I don't really need any sagebrush. No, sir, cactus is the only vegetation, practically, that it's got. And I've always had a theory that cactus is more like an animal than it is like a vege-table, anyhow. A cactus plant will go farther out of its way to do you dirt than a rattlesnake will. The snake will rattle first and give you a chance, but cactus will stab you in the dark without a word of warning. And a Gila monster or a horned toad is almost a vegetable compared to cactus, and a good-natured vegetable at that—almost a fruit, you might say.

"So I went out first, along with a couple of camera cowboys who were temporarily resting from their art. One of them was Roy Peters, who had originated in the wilds of New Jersey, where you've got to know how to ride hard and shoot straight—and Roy really had learned how to ride well enough, somewhere or other, for the film business. The other was Fred Parsons, and Fred was a genuine cow hand before he went and contaminated himself with romance and pictures. I hired horses to match their make-ups from old man Thompson, but he wouldn't rent me any cows.

"The day before Christmas the Colonel comes out, looking as kindhearted as Santa Claus, with this gift, whose name was Willis Hitchcock.

"When I saw Willis I liked him right off, and I was glad that this was a perfectly legitimate business deal he was going to have put across on him. Nothing shady, like that Colonel Elwood B. Sanford might have thought up if he had been operating alone, without my restraining conscience. Willis was between thirty-five and forty, and mighty pleasant, and full of innocent and eager curiosity about the West, like you are. He insisted on helping us get supper that night and clean up afterwards. He said he was crazy about roughing it like this, but he'd been so tied up in business and money-making ever since he left college that he'd never had a chance before. And old man Thompson and some of his hands came over after supper, and everybody talked West, West, West.

"Christmas Day, we didn't have either business or golf. We warmed up a couple of turkeys I'd bought in a Hollywood delicatessen store and opened up some bottles of drugstore cooking tonic, sherry type, which I get from an Italian grape ranch, and had a pioneer Christmas in the wilds—or, at least, Willis seemed to think it was.

"Next morning I got out my golf irons, for wooden clubs get all split up on my course, and put on some boots and chaps and handed some to Willis and the others. Thompson and some of his employees had come over, full of friendly curiosity, to be a gallery and put in a helping word when the sales talk seemed to need it; and Willis and Roy Peters and the Colonel and me were to be a foursome. Willis looked surprised at the boots and chaps.

" 'For golf?' he says.

"I saw right then it would be better to deal quite frankly with this problem at the start and get it over with. 'Once, Mr Hitchcock,' I said, 'I heard about a couple of rattlesnakes being seen in this neighborhood, and since then I've played golf in these things.'

" 'Yes,' says Colonel Elwood B. Sanford. 'Sometimes they come up here from the desert to spawn.' Then a sudden light came into the Colonel's eyes, like it does when a selling idea hits him with a rush. He was looking at old man Thompson, and I noticed that Thompson had on the rattlesnake-skin vest he sports when he wants to dress up special.

" 'Stacey,' says the Colonel, turning to me, 'I wish your rattlesnake crop was bigger and more dependable than it is, the prices they are bringing these days.'

"I wondered why rattlesnakes had become desirable all of a sudden; but Thompson seemed to be on. 'Your place would support a million of them, Major Stacey, if you only stocked and cultivated it the way I do mine,' says he.

" 'A million at ten dollars a pelt runs into money,' says the Colonel; and I cursed him in my heart for saying 'pelt.' I realized right then that he couldn't have had much experience in rural and pastoral salesmanship, only town stuff.

"But it didn't seem to make any difference to Willis; he was looking at the Colonel as if fascinated. 'And yet,' goes on the Colonel, 'it may be only a passing fad, that Mexican and South American craze for rattlesnake vests. By the time you'd harvested three or four million pelts the style might change and the market bust. After all, it's only a by-product.'

"We left it at that, to soak into Willis's mind, and went on to play the first hole. We wetted some sand with water from the canteens the boys carried, and teed up. You can't use these little wooden tees on my course, for they won't drive in anywhere, and I've never had any iron tees made for fear it might call attention to the nature of the soil.

"My first hole is a kind of a dog-leg hole. It's sort

of downhill in its general tendency for the first seven or eight hundred yards, and then you roll into an arroyo and turn to your right and follow the arroyo for quite a piece till you get to the green. And it's really green, too. There's a nice flat rock there that a mere child ought to be able to putt on, and I painted it green so as to make things seem more homelike and cozy.

"I've got a direction sign up at the brink of the arroyo. It says 'Pomegranate Boulevard' on it. I've got quite a lot of signs like that around my place. Once there was considerable excitement over selling it for a suburban development; it's only about forty miles from Los Angeles, the fastest-growing metropolis on this earth. I never could understand why that suburban project fell through, but when it did I used the street signs to mark out directions and greens. The first hole itself is at the corner of Pomegranate Boulevard and Geranium Avenue, where the modern high-school building was going to be, in one of the classiest residence sections.

" 'Do we drive right into that canyon?' asks Willis in surprise.

" 'That's not a canyon, that's just a little arroyo,' I informed him. 'We won't get to the canyon much before noon.'

"Willis drives off with his full iron, and the ball sails over two hundred yards before it hits the ground. Then it struck considerable of a declivity and rolled and bounded five or six hundred yards more and jumped

into the arroyo with the speed of a machine-gun bullet.
One nice thing about my golf course is that you can get
distance on the downhill holes, where the cactus isn't
too high—in fact, the ball wouldn't stop at all unless it
hit a hill or jumped into a gulch. I've made all my
downhill holes not more than par sevens and eights,
even when they're twelve or fifteen hundred yards long.
But the uphill holes run from par tens to par eighteens.

"When we got down into the arroyo we found the
balls had bursted open against the rocks on the far side.
But I've got a local rule that covers that. When a ball
bursts, you don't lose either stroke or distance, you just
tee up a new one and go ahead. We don't have any
earthquakes in this country, but we have temblors sometimes, and I've got another local rule that covers them
—anything a temblor does to ground you are playing
on makes it 'ground under repair,' and you are entitled
to lift out.

"We played around the bend of that dog-leg hole,
down towards the corner of Geranium Avenue and
Pomegranate Boulevard, and four or five times I heard
a buzzing and whirring, but Willis maybe didn't know
what that sound meant, for he didn't say anything. And
along the brink of the arroyo three or four coyotes were
slinking along watching us, and jumping out of sight
when I looked up at them, but I didn't call anybody's
attention to them. That hole is a natural centipede and
scorpion and tarantula hazard, and while I was still
three hundred yards away I saw the surface of the
green moving and waving, like straw with a breeze in

it. Hundreds of them were there, waving thousands of little legs, fighting and massacring each other.

"I slipped one of old man Thompson's men a niblick and told him to run ahead and clean it up, while I halted everybody by pretending I'd lost a ball. But pretty soon Willis noticed the man working and scraping with the niblick.

" 'What's he doing?' he asked, shading his eyes and staring at the green, three hundred yards away.

" 'Cleaning the chili grass off the green,' says the Colonel. 'It must have got the start of the Major during the rainy season.'

" 'Chili grass?' asks this Willis.

" 'Uh-huh,' says the Colonel. 'Chili grass. Just another by-product of this place, but you can't make chili con carne without it.'

"After a while the cow hand stopped work, and then in a minute I found that ball, and we played down to the green—this flat rock I was telling you about. When Willis putted into the hole, the ball rolled right out again; it was drifted almost full of sand.

" 'Hole's pretty shallow, Major,' complained Willis.

" 'Stacey don't dare sink 'em any deeper on this land,' says the Colonel, 'even when he sinks 'em into a flat rock like this. This rock's pretty thin, and it couldn't resist an awful lot of pressure.'

" 'What pressure is he afraid of?' says Willis, kind of puzzled—as I was myself.

" 'The pressure of the oil,' says the Colonel. 'It's liable to bust through anywhere here.' I knew by the look on his face and the way he drew in his breath that the real selling campaign was about to start.

" 'Is there oil here?' says Willis.

" 'Is there oil?' says the Colonel, in a kind of hushed and reverent voice. 'Is there oil?' And he took off his hat, like he was in church, or the national anthem was being played, or something.

" 'Oil,' he said. 'Oil!' And then all the natural poetry in that man's nature released itself. Willis and Thompson and the cowboys and me gathered round him in a circle, and it was like bells ringing across moonlit waters, and music playing, and childhood's happy days come back, and golden dreams of young love coming true and going on forever into the golden sunset of life —it was like that to listen to Colonel Elwood B. Sanford talk of the oil under that land of mine. He made even me believe in it.

"You're innocent, and you're Eastern, and in all your benighted life it's possible you never listened to an oil talk delivered by a born artist. I can't convey to you secondhand any of the solemn and almost religious feeling of it when it's put across properly. We have got beauty out here in this sun-kissed land of ours, the beauty of flowers and fruits and blue skies and glorious business opportunities and optimism and rejuvenated health, but there's no beauty anywhere in the world like the beauty of an oil talk when an old master like Colonel Elwood B. Sanford sweeps the strings of his angelic harp.

"I think he's a dirty old crook, on account of something I'll tell you later; but in some ways I've got to hand it to him. By the time he got through I was almost sobbing with uplift and patriotism and business possibilities, and I was crazy to buy that land myself. I would, too, if I hadn't been unfortunate enough to own it already.

"There was a kind of solemn stillness when he finished, and then one of the cowboys broke the tension by lighting a cigarette. He flipped the match, still burning, into the one and only greasewood shrub on my place. You may not know about greasewood. It don't so much take fire as it explodes.

" 'Just see that!' says the Colonel, as the greasewood plant flared up like two bushels of celluloid collars. 'This land is so full of oil that the plants suck it up; their roots are fairly swimming in it. You boys better be careful where you throw your matches after this.'

" 'But why don't you let the oil come up?' asks Willis; and it seemed a perfectly reasonable question to me.

" 'Major Stacey has been waiting until he could start his own refinery out here,' says the Colonel, 'so that other people wouldn't get the bulk of the profits.' And it sounded like a reasonable answer to me.

"This oil talk relieved my mind a good deal. Willis looked too intelligent to me to fall for the rattlesnake vests and the chili grass; although he'd said nothing. On the way to the second driving tee the Colonel mentioned potash, and that seemed reasonable, too. While we were playing the hole the Colonel sold Willis on the divots we took, which showed sulphur, copper, and borax, and that was all conservative enough.

"Then he got romantic again, when we pitched up onto the green. My second green is at the corner of what was going to be Orange Drive and Orchid Avenue. For some reason that's always been a popular street corner for Gila monsters to loaf around. Ever see a Gila monster? Well, he's a varmint that looks like he had wanted to be an alligator, but his growth had got stunted by lack of food, water, and public appreciation. He's sad about it, and the only noise he ever makes is like he was snoring. The cowboys had to boot a dozen of them out of the way before we could putt, and then get rid of a rattlesnake that was coiled in the cup itself.

"The Colonel sold the place on the desert crocodiles, as he called the Gila monsters, and the profit from their hides, and a little later he sold it again on a swarm of desert gnats we had to play through—bees that made desert honey, the sweetest in the world, from cactus, he said. I wished he'd quit saying 'desert' this and 'desert' that all the time, for I didn't want the word 'desert' to get drilled into Willis's consciousness.

"At the seventh hole, which is at the corner of Avocado Street and Chrysanthemum Terrace, he tried to palm off a convention of buzzards as eagles, and figured out for Willis what he'd make a year selling eagle feathers to the Indians. It didn't sound good to me. I wished he would stick to oil, which is dignified, conservative, and legitimate. The desert ticks and horseflies he snubbed entirely. He sold for a while on gold, iron, tin, radium, silver, magnesia, zinc, lead, and I felt a little safer, for there's lots of pretty-colored rock there.

"But I always will think he made a mistake when he tried to represent a coyote, which Willis saw galloping in the distance, as a sheep dog.

" 'Where are the sheep?' asked Willis.

"Just then a bunch of these long-tailed white rats that inhabit the desert trooped over a hill and down into an arroyo, and I yelled out quick to Willis, 'My sheep have all been sold and shipped.'

"For I saw in that Sanford's eye that he was going to try to represent those rats as desert lambs, or something. His mouth was open to do it. He closed his mouth and gave me an aggrieved look, like I was cramping his style, and then he opened his mouth again and sold those rats as desert foxes.

" 'There's a vitamin in the soil on the Major's place,' he said, 'that makes the fur of these Southern white foxes finer and silkier than the Northern species.'

"We were playing along the edge of the canyon itself then—as I recollect it, at the corner of Apricot Avenue and Riverbrink Drive—and the usual sandstorm was in progress there. You've always got to play through one to get into the canyon and to the tenth green, and to get out of it again by way of the eleventh, twelfth and thirteenth holes, which are sort of terraces, or shelves, or ledges, as you might say, on the far side. There's lots of climatic diversity on my place, but in the canyon itself there's only one season—that's the sandy season. Daytimes the sand washes out of the hills onto the desert near by, and nighttimes it washes back again.

" 'This sand,' says the Colonel, spitting a lot of it out and gasping, while we were putting on the tenth green, 'is the most valuable glass-making sand in the world. They send all the way from Europe for it, to make stained-glass windows for churches.'

" 'Uh-huh,' says Willis. 'Where's the water hole on this course?'

" 'There's a good water hole on my ranch not more than three or four miles from here,' says old man Thompson. 'If you were to decide to stock up with cows, I'd make an arrangement with you so your cattle could get water there.'

" 'Look here,' I said, 'you two are talking about different kinds of water holes. Mr Thompson means a water hole where cows drink, and Mr Hitchcock means a water hole where golfers lose balls.'

" 'Either would suit me right now,' says a cowboy, very tactless, I thought, blowing sand out of his nose.

" 'Isn't there any water on this place?' asks Willis.

"I'd been dreading that question. I'm going to trust you with a secret, now, that I wouldn't tell anybody but a close friend—the truth is, there *isn't* really much water on that land of mine. There; it's out now, and I feel better! I'm so candid and honest by nature that it worries me to conceal anything. Some former owner drove a well near the house, and there's a feeble little trickle of water can be pumped out with a gasoline engine. There's as much gasoline goes into the engine, nearly, as water comes out of the well. When I first got the place, which I took on a bad debt I never could have collected anyhow, I rigged up a shower bath back of the 'dobe house. But when you turn the shower on, the last couple of years, nothing comes out but spiders, ticks, and ants; and now and then a little baby centipede.

"The Colonel, stung to desperation, pointed to a streak of white sand at the top of one of the hills and began to orate about the perpetual snow of the mountains and how it fed the perpetual springs.

"'I don't see any springs anywhere,' said Willis, with his back to the way the wind was blowing from.

"'Turn round!' yells the Colonel; and we all looked where he was pointing. Five or six horned toads, that had been blown in from the desert with the sand, were sitting on a rock, and they began to hop away as the Colonel approached them.

"'You see those frogs?' says the Colonel. 'Just follow the frogs and you'll come to the springs and marshland!'

"And while we played the rest of the way out of that canyon and its perpetual sandstorm, the Colonel wheezed and spluttered and sold the property on frog legs, figs, and oranges.

"Before we played the fourteenth hole, which is located at the corner of Date Palm Place and Waterlily Close, we rested a little and got the sand out of our eyes with water from the canteens. Then we teed up and drove off for the fifteenth hole. The fifteenth hole is like this: First, you've got to go over a little hill, which has a flat place on top of it, and then down the other side to the green. You can't see the green, which is at the corner of Almond Street and Narcissus Boulevard, until you get to the top of the hill. There's a kind of a little depression in the flat place at the top of the hill. It's rocky and warm up there, and some days quite a few of my snakes are lolling around in order to get caressed by the sun.

"Just as we got to the top of the hill, 'Crack!' went a rifle somewhere, and 'Ping!' went a bullet over our heads.

"Without any conference among us, we all flung ourselves with one accord into the dip in the ground, just as there rang out one of those wild, unearthly yells, fierce and mournful, that nobody but an Indian has ever been able to tear out of his vocal cords.

"I risked an eye over the edge of the hollow we'd all dropped into. It was who I thought it might be— Mojave Dave. Dave was down on the putting green, with a chuckwalla he had been eating in one hand, and a rifle in the other, doing one of those dances you usually got to pay money to see. He'd eat some chuckwalla, and then he'd yell another yell, and then he'd cut another caper, and then he'd let loose another bullet; and it wasn't a civilized sight at all for anybody to see that you were trying to sell property to.

" 'Where did old Dave get hold of a rifle?' asked one of Mr Thompson's cow hands, who had also been risking an eye.

" 'It's mine—the old varmint's made himself a Christmas present of it,' said Mr Thompson, clawing at a tick that had worked its way into his skin through his whiskers. 'Don't you boys remember I missed my rifle a couple of days ago, and five boxes of ca'tridges?'

" 'Five boxes—huh! That's two hundred and fifty shots Dave's got,' says the cow hand.

"Dave, he let out another yell and another bullet. It hit a small stone, and the stone jumped, and ricocheted, and hit Willis in the nose, and the blood spurted. And just then I heard a familiar kind of a buzzing somewhere near, and take it all in all it didn't look like such a good sales argument for my property. We didn't dare to stand up, or even lift ourselves high enough to crawl away downhill, the bullets were coming so fast and steady just an inch above us; we had to lie there among the insects while the pebbles danced around us.

" 'Those golf balls must have bounced down at Dave over the hill, while he was eating his dinner,' said old man Thompson. 'You boys should have yelled "Fore." '

"Dave is really a nice old fellow, and I never heard of his acting that foolish, excited way before. The only thing the matter with him is that he gets loco spells.

"Dave lives mostly in the desert, and what he lives on is chuckwallas and canned peaches. You don't know what a chuckwalla is? Well, it ain't like a peach. Dave inhabits my place a good deal because of there being more of his favorite game animals on it than any place of similar size in the world.

"His canned peaches he gets mostly from Thompson and me. Old Dave is loco on the subject of owning all the land there is, anywhere. He's a Mojave, but he don't live with any tribe or village; and he says he's the only Indian left that never had anything to do at any time with a government reservation. He says the Indians once owned the whole country, and him being the only ungovernmented Indian remaining, why, naturally, he is the heir to everything everywhere.

"But Dave is usually right reasonable about it, too. He'll trade. He sells the land every so often. About every six weeks Thompson buys his ranch from Dave all over again with another can of peaches, and I guess I've purchased my place from him fifty times in the last five or six years. Once I asked him why I had to keep on and on buying it from him.

"'Dave,' I says, 'you ought to stick to a bargain when you make it.' 'Huh!' says he. 'No! Dave no stick! Dave heap like white man!' But Thompson and I like him, and we were both surprised to see him misbehaving this way. Before this his wrongs had only made him sort of sad and dignified, and not active.

"I saw Fred Parsons reach for his gun.

"'Here,' I said, 'don't you shoot at Dave! He's a friend of mine. He's got the heart of a child. He'll be all right as soon as those ca'tridges are all shot away.'

"Fred took a 'Bang! Bang!' over the lip of the depression we were lying in; and in a second I heard something thrashing about among the pebbles.

" 'Excuse me, Major Stacey,' says Fred, 'but I didn't have time to explain before I shot. I wasn't shooting at the Indian. I was just nicking that rattlesnake that had reared himself up there like he was going to kiss Mr Hitchcock on the neck.'

"There was another whirring that made us all feel like we ought to rise from that little hollow. And some more bullets and dancing stones that made us feel like we better keep on lying down.

" 'You take my gun, Mr Thompson,' says Roy Peters, handing it over; 'you can probably shoot better than I can.'

"So old man Thompson lay on our right flank shooting the heads off of rattlesnakes when they lifted above the edge of the hollow, and Fred Parsons lay on the left flank doing a similar humanitarian work. The pebbles poor old Dave kicked up bounced amongst us, and his bullets whined above us and spattered around us, and I saw a couple of buzzards idling about above as if they were looking for business opportunities, and on the whole it was one of the most nervous and irritating golf games I ever implicated myself in.

"Just as I was wondering how Willis was enjoying all this, I heard him laugh.

" 'Say, Colonel Sanford,' he says, 'just exactly what is the advantage of Indians on a place like this?'

" 'Advantage!' yells the Colonel. 'Indians!' And in his excitement he sat up to orate. One of Dave's little

Yuletide greetings combed his chin beard, and he lay down again. But from where he lay, he started the most outrageous selling talk I ever listened to.

"Sell? What did he sell? Why, sir, he sold that Indian himself! Sold him while he dodged his bullets. Sold him romantic and sold him commercial! I only wish I could think that man Sanford is as honest as he is talented. He lay there in the hot sand with ticks in his neck and horseflies under his collar and tried to turn that total loss that was plunking bullets at us into a glorious asset.

" 'Mr Hitchcock,' he yells, above the din and rattle of the bombardment, 'Mr Hitchcock, you are fortunate in witnessing the last Indian uprising this country will ever see, fortunate in being in the midst of a historic moment. . . .'

"He smashed a centipede with his boot and discouraged a Gila monster with his mashie, and went right on:

"—'Chief Bear Skin down there is greeting us with all the beautiful, untamed enthusiasm of his race, but he is really happy! Happy because he and his tribe have consummated a deal with Major Stacey whereby the Major is to take charge of marketing all the Indian products. . . .'

"His broad hat floated away on the wind of one of Dave's bullets, for he'd raised his head too high again.

"—'Indian products,' yelled the Colonel, as his hat left him. 'Blankets, metalwork, beads, pottery, baskets.

There's a fortune in it, Mr Hitchcock, there's a fortune. . . .'

"A flying pebble knocked his false teeth out, but he rescued them from a chuckwalla, wiped them on his sleeve, put them in again, gulped, and went right on. . . .

"—'This fortune, Mr Hitchcock, will be yours! For we offer you the Indian contract with the land! All aboriginal rights and all riparian rights go with the property, Mr Hitchcock, making it the most desirable purchase in all the Golden West!'

"Yes, sir; I wish from the bottom of my heart that man had probity to match his gifts!

"Suddenly, I got an idea. 'Dave,' I yelled, sticking up my head at the risk of getting my toupee mussed up. 'Dave! Peaches! Peaches!'

"Thompson caught the idea, too, and began to yell: 'Peaches, Dave, peaches!' And the rest of them joined in without knowing why they were doing it.

"Dave, he had a box of ca'tridges left, and he looked at 'em wishful. And he listened wishful to the cry of 'Peaches!' He stood doubtful for a minute, but the desire for some dessert after his dinner conquered his sense of his wrongs, and he dropped his gun and came towards us. We all got up.

" 'There's four cans in my shack,' I says to one of Thompson's cowboys. 'Take him over and give them all to him!'

"Just then Fred Parsons let out a yell. 'Great Jehoshaphat!' he said and pointed.

"We looked where he was pointing, and there was the city of Los Angeles!

"A mirage, like we sometimes have in the desert countries, was showing it to us as if it were only five or six miles away—this wonderful city, which will have between two and three million inhabitants the next census count if we ain't crooked out of it somehow, with all its skyscrapers and spires reaching up into the blue, unclouded heavens! Near! Why, it looked so near you felt like you could reach right over into Hollywood and put your hand onto the new First National Bank or John Barrymore.

"Colonel Elwood B. Sanford stuck out his hands towards it like he had created it himself and loved it.

" 'Look!' he said, with that magnificent gesture. 'The city is coming nearer to this fine suburban development every day! From the corner of Almond Street and Narcissus Boulevard, where we stand now, a new car line will soon run right down to the center of Los Angeles proper! It will be but fifteen minutes from here to the Southern Pacific Railway station.'

"I've heard men sell almost everything; but he was the first optimist I ever knew personally who tried to sell a mirage. And yet, in the midst of my admiration, there crept a little doubt. He had genius, but genius can blunder. It takes genius to stand in the midst of a passel of dead rattlesnakes, with a loco Indian beside you, and buzzards drifting inquisitive towards you, and sell these critters as desirable suburban improvements for a city forty miles away. It's genius, but is it sound? Is it judgment? For you can only sell a mirage as long as it lasts.

" 'I didn't know it was so near,' says Willis.

" 'I brought you around the long way purposely,' says the Colonel. 'I wanted you to get a look at the scenery, and I was saving this as a surprise for you.'

"But sure enough, it was a blunder. It was super-salesmanship, but it wasn't sense.

"For right in the midst of the most eloquent suburban lot sale I ever hearkened to, that dream city winked sarcastic at us—and faded out.

"At the same moment a chill came out of the canyon, and I heard an owl screech in the hills, and a coyote began to sing somewhere a long way off in an arroyo. Willis laughed, and then he shuddered a little, too; and if I ever saw the face of a man that felt oversold, his was it. We all went back to the shack for supper, me wishing every step of the way the Colonel had concentrated on oil and minerals. Oil always seems reasonable and sound and conservative.

"I hope you're my friend. I couldn't bear to tell the rest of this to anyone that wasn't full of sympathetic friendship.

"Well, after supper a trifling little ten-cent-limit poker game got itself started; and I wish I could remember for sure whether it was Colonel Elwood B. Sanford that proposed it. Anyhow—

"You've got a guess as to what that chill wind blew out of the canyon in the way of luck. I state with shame that it was I myself who suggested that the limit of this game be raised to a quarter. It was old man Thompson that wanted it hiked to fifty cents. It was Roy Peters who thought it ought to be a dollar limit afterwhile. I don't remember that this Willis Hitchcock ever suggested any hiking at all. It was Fred Parsons who said he liked stud poker better than draw.

"The day after Christmas, when this game started, was a Wednesday. Along towards Thursday evening Thompson left us, with my car, and when he came back he brought two cases of something he said was drinkable, and he found us playing four-dollar stud with an eight-dollar bet on the last card.

"On Friday, the cowboys of the Thompson outfit, who had long since been cleaned out, thought they'd better bid us adiós and go and look after cattle a little.

"What I especially remember about Saturday is that some time that day the limit of this game faded away just like that mirage had. There wasn't any limit any more. By Sunday evening this Willis Hitchcock had a check for everything I had in the bank, two building lots in Pasadena, the car I come up there in, another brand-new car in a garage in Hollywood, a half interest in a store building in Beverly Hills, an IOU for the value of a hundred head of cattle that was once Thompson's, everything that Colonel Elwood B. Sanford said he possessed, and a half interest in that very property we were sitting playing on and had tried so hard to sell him. I say nothing of further IOU's ad nauseum.

"You know what I think, mister? I think, somewhere

about the middle of that game, or nearer its start, that Sanford person deserted my flag and made common cause with this Willis Hitchcock. And later went and shared what this Willis Hitchcock took from me. The way some of those hands was dealt and played makes me more and more suspicious the more I think 'em over.

"It was the day after New Year's. Willis said he guessed he'd have to bid us good-by, and he went down to the road and climbed into the car I'd come up there in, and then he says:

" 'Major, would you like to cut the cards just once more before I start? One half of this place against the other half?'

"We cut. I hoped I'd lose—that darned place and trying to sell it had cost me so much money that I wanted to be rid of it all and never hear of it again. But I won his half of it back, and that made me wonder if he wasn't a slicker with cards. There I was, stuck with it all once more!

" 'Well,' says Willis, turning on the ignition and starting the engine, 'I certainly have enjoyed my little golfing trip up here. And when any of you boys come down to Tia Juana you must make a point of looking me up.'

" 'Tia Juana!' I said. 'Aren't you from the East?'

" 'Why, no,' says Willis. 'I was born and brought up right in Los Angeles.'

" 'Aren't you a retired banker?' I asks.

" 'Yes,' he says. 'I am. I mostly fool around with horses and other games now. It's been quite a while since I had anything to do with a faro bank. Good-by, boys!' And with that he let in the clutch and was off.

"I can't find it in my heart to think that Colonel Elwood B. Sanford knew he was a professional gambler and planted him on me from the start. If so, why would he have tried to sell that land so hard? And he really tried—I could tell. No, the thought of turning and rending me came to the Colonel after that game got started."

Major Stacey fell into a sad silence, which I respected. He rolled himself another cigarette and looked bluely at the blue smoke. Presently he spoke:

"There's just one little thing that might be construed as consolation. Colonel Sanford owns half that land now. Us losers had a few consolation rounds, and he won it. And someday he'll go up there with another prospect, and fall off a cliff, or get stung by a rattlesnake, or something. He will, if there's any justice in the universe, on account of the trick he played me."

One of the Japanese bellboys came out of the hotel. "Telephone for you, Major Stacey," he said.

The Major went in, and it was ten minutes before he returned. There was a queer look on his face, as if he didn't know whether to be glad or sorry.

"That phone call was from old man Thompson," he said, "and I'm trying to figure whether there's justice in the universe or not. This morning one of his hands slung a stick of dynamite at a family of rattlesnakes in the bottom of that canyon, and the explosion opened up

an oil gusher—and that old grafter, Colonel Elwood
B. Sanford, owns half that oil!"

He sat down, and frowned, and smiled, and smiled
and frowned. Finally he said:

"It's terrible on a man like me, who has always led
a life of honesty and idealism, to be hooked up as a
business partner with an old crook like Colonel Elwood
B. Sanford! I wonder if I couldn't buy his half of that
property right now—before he finds out about the oil."

And he went into the telephone booth again.

SHE TELLS THE REPORTER

I SUPPOSE I might as well tell you everything, for you tabloid reporters are going to print something anyhow, and the same holds good with pictures. I might as well give you one, or you will print something; and That Woman has told you her side of the case and filled you up with lies and handed you her picture, and you might as well know the truth about it.

Well, Eddie worked in the same office where I was a stenog, and I met him right after I came out of business college. He took me to the pictures several times, and I could not but admire his refined tastes. He had a refined sense of humor and would always josh the titles, and dialogue after the talkies came in, and we would always have a good time looking at the same.

One day I said to him, just for a joke, "Suppose you are married, Mr Bates?"

He kind of surprised me. He said, "In name only. I consider myself absolved from that Ball and Chain."

He explained it was just a Boyish Prank to begin with, and now she was going around with boy friends. In a lot of ways Eddie Bates is just a great big boy, and if you knew him personal you would realize the same.

He said to me, "Gertie, I will Consummate a Divorce, and marry you." This was one afternoon when we was looking at a Greta Garbo, and Eddie says:

"Kid, her and you are my Ideals. My Dream Girls!"

But when he consummated his divorce from his first wife he married his present wife—That Woman—and I reproached him for doing so one night when he called at our house.

"Gertie," he said, "it was kind of unexpected to me, too. She dared me, Sally did. You would not want a man so weak-spirited he could not take a Dare, would you, Girlie? A man has got to live his own life."

I could see that okay, but my parents thought I ought to give Eddie up, but it would of broke our hearts. From the first he always said I was his One Ideal Woman. Sally is really The Other Woman, for Eddie and I were fated for each other. It has been Kismet.

When he married Sally I was afraid sooner or later I and he would begin to drift apart. My parents kept on saying now he was married again why should he keep on calling on me and stay so late? But I said: "You are the Older Generation; you do not understand."

They persecuted me and made my home a hell to me. "A dawn will come when you will not find me here," I told them.

I thought I ought to go and have a heart-to-heart talk with That Woman who called herself Eddie's wife, and show her there was Ideals in the world, and something a good deal Higher to live up to, but she would act so snippy with me.

You see, she worked in the same office with I and Eddie, and when we would leave the office together she would make scenes. Sally never had any sense of refinement.

This practically illegal Matrimony between the two of them, which had no Higher Ideals in it, went on and on till it resulted in the cutest little baby. Eddie always carried a picture of it, and he would call it by my name, Gertie, when he showed me the picture.

But Sally, that Other Woman, who dares to call herself by the sacred name of Wife, made him call it by her name when she was around. She had one of those vulgar, jealous dispositions and continually showed the same.

She tried in every underhanded way to win Eddie away from me. She used to try to horn in sometimes when I and Eddie would go out to lunch or dinner together. I could never be sold on That Woman. Once she came to our house when Eddie was calling, and it was very embarrassing, for she has no finer feelings and does not appear to want the same.

The way she acted when she called gave my parents a talking point against me, and they kept on making my home a hell. Oh, dear, the world is such a hard place for a girl!

Finally I went last Tuesday evening to her house and told her she was an attempted interloper between I and Eddie, and he was mine by all the Higher Laws, and if she was anything like a square shooter she would give him up to me and not try to separate us, and tried to show her what wickedness it was to try to keep two hearts away from each other that beat as one, like I and Eddie's.

She got nasty then and attacked me in the most impudent way, for she has no refinement, and Eddie came in just then, and she attacked him. I did not see her hit him with the bottle, as I was leaving to avoid a vulgar scene, and I hope it is going to be a concussion and not a fracture of the brain, for I love him so.

If he was to die from it the world would be bleak to me. But if he gets over it, I and him both will be strengthened by suffering, and That Woman will be out of our lives forever, soon after, I trust.

And if you got to print my picture I wouldn't want it printed right next to hers; maybe you could tell the editor to put a picture of each of us on each side of the picture of him, and if you should print the baby's picture you ought to call it Gertie, for that is what Eddie calls it, and if it should turn out to be a fracture instead of only a concussion you would be obeying poor Eddie's last wish if you was to call it Gertie.

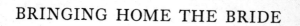

BRINGING HOME THE BRIDE

THANK you, Freddy, I *will* have a little scotch, now that you suggest it. And I wonder if I could sleep here to-night, on the couch in your living room? You see, I can't go to my own flat.

No, Freddy, I have not been evicted. Some other people are living in it. There's no room for me. I took them in because they had no place to go and were hungry and thirsty. I was in to see them yesterday, and they seemed to be doing their best to assuage their hunger and thirst. My little store of wet and dry groceries is rapidly disappearing. When I mentioned it, they threw me out. They said that I had cost them millions and millions of dollars, and if they stayed there a thousand years and used my supplies all the time, it would only be a small partial payment on what I had lost for them.

I could stand being a homeless wanderer, but their ingratitude wounds me. I am too tenderhearted for my own good. If I were not tenderhearted I would not be in all this trouble.

It all started at a floor show. No, not a flower show; a floor show. They are quite different. A flower show is all perfume and dew; and a floor show is all perfume and perspiration.

Bertie Duffield and I were having dinner at one of

these places which has a floor show one day last week, and Bertie was very melancholy, so I sent for the bartender and gave him instructions as to how to make the Henry Withersbee cocktail. It is a cocktail I invented and named after myself during Prohibition days, and I saw no reason to give it up after Repeal.

So I said, "This will cheer you up, if anything will, Bertie."

"Thank you, Henry," he said, after we had had a couple of them. "Isn't it queer how floor shows get started in places that have scarcely any floor?"

There was a man dancing with a girl and swinging her around and around; and I had an idea she was a very pretty girl, but she was going round and round so fast I couldn't be sure.

"Probably," said Bertie, "the headwaiter or somebody says to the proprietor, 'Let's have a floor show!' and the proprietor or somebody says, 'Goody! Goody! Let's.' And they hire it, and then find out they haven't any floor to speak of; and it just squirms around underfoot."

So we had some more of the Withersbee cocktails, and I said to him, "Bertie, you can't fool me; you are very sad about something. Won't you tell me everything? After all, we are each other's oldest and best friends."

"They might put it on the ceiling," said Bertie, looking up at the ceiling. "Like spiders." So he called the headwaiter and said: "A floor show on the ceiling would be quite a novelty. Everybody in town would soon be talking about it, and the place would be crowded."

The man looked terribly stupid, so I explained to him, "Like spiders, you know."

All the time this girl was going round and round and round, and I wished she would stop so I could see whether she was really very pretty or not. Such portions of her as came to my attention as she whirled looked quite attractive.

"What is there in them, Henry?" Bertie asked.

"Ingredients," I said. "The first thought I had was gin; then a friend gave me a case of rum; and I already had some whisky. So I got some bitters, and then some people were at my flat one night and suggested some brandy. The idea sort of grew and grew. The champagne was my own notion. It seems to me that you are not as sad as you were, Bertie."

"I choke back my grief, Henry," he said. "But I bleed inwardly. My father doesn't like me any more."

"I didn't know he ever did," I said.

"I thought for a long time that was only a pose on his part," said Bertie. "He was making a bluff at not liking me, so as to get me to go to work at something. But it now appears that he was sincere in it all the time. He is now speaking of disinheriting me unless I go to work."

I thought of this very seriously, while I watched this girl whirling. All of a sudden, the man who was whirling her let loose of her, and she skeeted right across the floor and brought up against me.

"That's right," I said to the man, "get her all perspiring and then throw her at me! I don't think you know me well enough to do a thing like that."

But Bertie said to the girl, "Hello, Sugar!"

"Hello, Bertie darling!" she said to him. But he only sighed and looked more melancholy than ever. And Sugar went back to dancing and being whirled again.

"Well," I said to Bertie, "why *don't* you get a job? Your father is right. You are wasting your life. You ought to reform. Why shouldn't you get a job and amount to something?"

"I can only say to you what I said to my father, Henry," said Bertie. "My sense of honor won't let me get a job. I've got too much social conscientiousness to get a job."

"Where did you get that from?" I asked him.

"I keep up with the times," he said. "With millions of people needing jobs badly, how would it look for the son of the wealthy Albert Duffield to take work away from some poor fellow and doom his wife and family to destitution and starvation? Despicable, I should call it!"

"Have you explained that to your father?" I asked him.

"He won't talk to me. He won't even see me," said Bertie. "I am terribly fond of my father, but his gray hairs are hounding me in sorrow to my grave. I wonder if I don't know those girls?"

"What girls?" I asked him.

"Those girls that keep going round and round all the time," he said.

"There is only one girl going round and round all the time," I said.

"Are you quite sure of that, Henry?" he said.

"Oh, quite," I said. "She looks like two sometimes, but when the man let loose of her and she skeeted over here it was very apparent that there was only one of her."

"Well, thank heaven for that!" said Bertie with a sigh. "That's something that's right, anyhow."

"What difference does it make whether there's one of her or two of her?" I said.

"It avoids possible complications," said Bertie. "You see, I think I know her pretty well."

"What you need," I said, "is a manager, Bertie. You need to put all your affairs in the hands of someone who would start in by reforming you, and who would reconcile you to your father. A longheaded, capable, experienced man of the world."

Bertie looked at me very intently for two or three minutes, and then he leaned across the table and said:

"Henry, would *you* do it?"

I did not hesitate an instant. Here was an old friend —my best friend—in need. I knew that he could trust me; and I knew that I had just the tact for the job. To reconcile Bertie with his father would take tact. I knew the old gentleman, and I felt that he regarded me as a steady character, and if I told him that I was reforming Bertie, and setting him a good example, the rest would be easy. He knew me as a man of experience in the business world. He very nearly gave me a job, right after Bertie and I left college, selling bonds; which showed that he had a high notion of my stability and trustworthiness. Mr Duffield has something to do with banks, and with life insurance companies, and I have heard that he was interested in oil and rubber; and if a man like that almost gives you a job, it is because he has discerned great trustworthiness and ability in you. If he had seen it when I was a raw youth, just out of college, how much more would he be impressed now that I had had seven or eight years of contact with the world! These thoughts ran through my mind like wildfire, and I felt that I held Mr Duffield in the hollow of my hand.

"We will go and see him at once," I said.

"See whom?" said Bertie. He was staring at the dancing girl again. "Henry," he said, "I am afraid that there *are* two of them after all!"

"See Mr Duffield. See your father," I said. "I hold him in the hollow of my hand."

"Oh, him," he said. "I don't think it's any use. And there *are* two of them! That makes it all the worse."

"Where will we find your father now?" I said, holding him to the point. For when I have a matter of importance to put through, I am all speed and decision.

"The family's in Westchester this summer," said Bertie.

"Let's go," I said.

But outside the restaurant, Bertie stopped me as I was about to hail a taxicab.

"We'll go in this," he said and pointed to a station

wagon at the curb. "That's what I came here in." It seems that the last time he had seen his father, Bertie had driven up to Westchester and had traded his car, which was a little roadster, to his father for this station wagon, which was more convenient if you should suddenly get the notion to take quite a number of people on a party. And when his father had found out about the trade, it had made him more determined than ever that what Bertie needed was to be disinherited.

So we got in and started for Westchester, and pretty soon Bertie said, "Fifth Avenue reminds me of Texas."

I couldn't see that at all, so I asked him why.

"Because, no matter where you are going," said Bertie, "once you have crossed Texas, you are halfway there."

"It seems to me," I said, "that we have crossed Fifth Avenue several times. You don't suppose that indicates we have been there and are coming back again?"

"I believe you are right," said Bertie; "about there being only one of them."

Then I noticed that Sugar was with us. So I said, "If you are as confused as all that, I had better do the driving from now on, Bertie."

And this girl Sugar made a remark which showed her to be a very sensible woman. She said, "If you are going to Westchester, why not just stick to driving along Fifth Avenue for a while, instead of crossing it all the time?"

I saw in a flash that she was right. So Sugar said that every time she had driven into Westchester she had crossed a bridge somewhere. But Bertie said, no, that bridge was when you went to New Jersey. I had a distinct recollection myself that it was when you went out on Long Island that you crossed a bridge. So I said that Sugar had better do the driving, and that Bertie could look out on one side for bridges, and I would look out on the other. For it dawned on me like an inspiration that the success of the whole enterprise depended on going over the right bridge. And I did not think Bertie could be trusted. He seemed to be a little sleepy, so I had Sugar stop the station wagon, and I went into a place and had several flasks of the Withersbee cocktail compounded. It seemed to waken Bertie up for a moment and then make him sleepier than ever. But that was all right with me. For I knew that I would have to do all the talking when we got to Mr Duffield's place, and I was glad to have Bertie quiet, for I felt that if he began to chatter he would spoil everything.

"Everything," I said to Sugar, "depends on the impression we make on Mr Duffield. Bertie's future depends on it—and everything."

So Sugar said, that was one reason she had come along. She thought she had quite a way with elderly gentlemen; and anyhow, the best plan was to take the plunge and get it over with.

Sugar said she thought we must be getting near a bridge, for we were near a string of big open markets, where everybody was buying everything. And she had noticed a lot of markets like that one time before when she had driven to Westchester.

So I said, "Stop!" And Sugar stopped.

"The idea of this trip is to please Mr Duffield, isn't it?" I said. "Well, then, what could put him in a better humor than a well-selected present?"

Sugar agreed with me that it was a splendid idea, but what would a well-selected present be?

"Use your mind, Sugar," I said. "Don't go through life just getting by on your beauty. Mr Duffield is a gentleman of rural tastes, otherwise he wouldn't have an estate in the country. A well-selected present would be something rural, of course."

So Sugar looked at the market and said, what could be more rural than chickens? There were some live ones in crates, and there was an extraordinary number of people buying things. Colored people seemed to predominate; but there were other people who were not colored, and some you could not swear to one way or the other. So to be certain, we waked Bertie up, and Sugar said, "How does your father like chickens, Bertie?"

"Fried," said Bertie and went to sleep again.

That gave me an inspiration, and I went into a place out of which a lot of music was coming, and people were eating and drinking and dancing in there, mostly colored people. Everybody knows they fry chickens better than anyone else in the world. So I said to Sugar that we would take old Mr Duffield the best colored chicken fryer in New York, and that would please him. And we danced a while in there, Sugar and I, while Bertie and the live chickens snored and cackled out at the curb in the station wagon, and Sugar said we had better stick to the Withersbee cocktails we had brought with us, for who could tell what you might be drinking in this dump?

So we hired a very large cook named Caroline. She was quite extensive and dark and heavy, and we put her in with Bertie. We were delayed a little, for Caroline had to stop and get a bundle and a little mulatto boy, and the little mulatto boy had a dog, and we put them all in with Bertie. And then Sugar asked Caroline if she could cook ducks, too? And Caroline said she could, but fish was what she prided herself on.

So at the next market we got a crate of live ducks and some fish. The fish were not alive, but they were very raw, and the little mulatto boy's dog and the ducks seemed somehow to be very much excited over the fish and each other, and then I made a great discovery. I discovered from interrogating the little mulatto boy that Caroline was a great rabbit cook, also. She had been too modest to say so, it seems. So we got three crates of live rabbits. It was getting so crowded inside that we got the men who sold us the rabbits to put all the crates on top of the station wagon and tie them on with ropes.

Sugar found a bridge pretty soon, and she said, "If Bertie's father isn't pleased with these presents, he must be a very crusty old gentleman indeed."

A traffic cop asked us when we went through White Plains if we weren't kind of top-heavy, and Sugar asked him if White Plains wasn't the place where George Washington had camped out during the war.

"What's that got to do with your drivin' intoxicated?" says the cop. "I've got a notion to run you in."

Sugar explained that she wasn't intoxicated; what he smelled was Bertie and the fish, and she told him that if he had an ounce of patriotism in him he wouldn't think of stopping her.

She said, "You must be a British sympathizer!"

"What makes you say that?" said the cop, getting red in the face.

"You act like it," she said. And they had quite a lengthy and heated conversation, because he was Irish and bitterly resented being called an English sympathizer.

"What makes you say I act like it?" he said.

"Keeping the supplies away from General Washington's camp," said Sugar. And they had quite a complicated argument about that, and in the end he let us go to square himself with Sugar.

The little mulatto boy had got the notion somewhere that General Washington was dead, and began to weep passionately and kick Caroline on the shins and ask her where he was being taken to, claiming that he had no intention of going where dead men and ghosts were; and his unseemly racket woke Bertie up.

The Henry Withersbee cocktail is not an ordinary drink. It goes right down to the psychic roots of a man's being. It did this with Bertie now. I had given up all thought of Bertie being any use as a guide to his

father's estate—but, presto! Two more of the Withersbee cocktails, and there was Bertie telling Sugar
what turns to take, and where to go, and, queerly
enough, telling her right. He was speaking out of a
kind of trance. The Withersbee cocktail had once more
wrought its wonders on the psychic parts of man.

We passed thousands of miles of shrubbery, and then
Sugar missed some goal posts or gateposts or something, and Bertie said, "Here we are!"

"Where are we, Bertie?" I asked, because I could
not see anything in any direction but these barbered
evergreens—you know what I mean, Freddy. They clip
these hedges into queer shapes, the way you clip a dog
to make him look like a lion. There was moonlight
floating over everything, as if it were a mist, and the
moonlight was all mixed up with this queer-shaped
shrubbery, and it made it seem as if the shrubbery were
floating, too—all those odd-looking monsters loomed
over us, Freddy, and it makes me shudder even now to
think of it. I think I had better have a drink. I shuddered at the time, though it was a warm summer evening. It was funereal. The little mulatto boy screamed
out to Caroline, "Oh, Mammy, Mammy, you've took
me to the place where the dead men live!"

I could quite sympathize with him; and Sugar said to
me, "I hope Bertie never asks me to come out here to
live!"

"Why should he ask you to?" I said.

"Well, he might," said Sugar. "You see, we got
married day before yesterday."

"I told you," said Bertie, "that I was almost certain I knew who those girls were."

"You keep saying 'those girls,' Bertie," I said to him. "There's only one of them, I tell you."

"Well, you know now why I was so glad there turned out to be only one," said Bertie. "There's going to be enough trouble over one. I don't know what would happen if I brought home two brides at the same time."

Sugar claimed we were in some kind of a driveway and suggested that if we kept on going we might come to a house. And Bertie said, oh, certainly, that had often happened to him, and in this very driveway, too. He often came to a house. And in a minute more Sugar said that she heard human voices and saw lights off through the animals—through the shrubbery, I mean. They must have heard us coming, too, for the chickens and ducks had got quite excited over something, and the dog was barking, and the rabbits were squeaking, and the little mulatto boy was howling, and Caroline was making a great to-do over spanking him and reassuring him about going where General Washington and the other dead men lived.

Bertie said, "My poor Father! My poor dear Mother! They've been terribly alarmed—they are waiting up for me!" He began to cry. "I'm an undutiful son," he said, "to cause them so much anxiety!"

"They will be tickled pink," I said, "when they realize that you have reformed, and a new life has begun for you." For I saw that I would have to stress that note a great deal in effecting this reconciliation.

"How long do you suppose they have been waiting up?" Sugar asked him.

"Since February, Sugar," said Bertie. "I haven't seen them since February."

"And here it is June," said Sugar.

"Time certainly does fly, don't hit, Miss Sugar!" said Caroline.

Just then we came to a terrace, and there were quite a lot of people sitting out on the terrace, all in evening clothes, and they had been drinking coffee. I am an extremely acute observer, and I twigged at once that some sort of party had been going on—probably a dinner party, and they had come out to the terrace for their coffee. They all seemed to be terribly solemn, stern-looking people, both men and women. They stared frigidly at us when Sugar stopped the station wagon at the terrace. Something seemed to hold them motionless, and I could sympathize with the little mulatto boy when he sang out to Caroline:

"Oh, Mammy, Mammy—the dead people! There they are! The dead people! Take me home! Take me home!"

The poor little fellow was so alarmed and excited that he was wiping his eyes with a fish.

I think quickly in emergencies. It came to me with the speed of lightning that the first impression must be a fortunate one—I must get in the first punch, so to speak. So I got out of the station wagon and said to Mr Duffield, whom I remembered very well:

"Mr Duffield, I have come out to tell you that Bertie

is a reformed character. He is leading a new life, Mr Duffield—married and settled down and steadied, and everything. I have brought him along, and his bride, too."

A handsome, middle-aged lady, who I learned later was Bertie's mother, caught at her breast and said, "The bride! Good heavens! Now that boy has gone and married some terrible woman!"

The little mulatto boy had slipped out of the car and was standing by one of the wheels. I think myself it was a diplomatic error to bring him along, and if Bertie had consulted me I should have discouraged the idea. The fish with which he had been wiping his eyes was in his hand, and now he cried out, "Don't you call my mammy a terrible woman! My mammy is a nice lady, you ol' dead white woman, you!" And with that he socked Mrs Duffield with the fish—"socked" is the only word, Freddy. It made a noise which sounded like the word "socked." I felt at the time that it was a painful incident, and I still think so. Pour me a drink, Freddy. I am still a little unnerved at the recollection.

The little mulatto boy's exclamation, I fancy, gave Bertie's parents a false impression. They could scarcely be blamed for thinking the little mulatto boy might possibly be their grandchild, or their step-grandchild, or something of that sort. Caroline leaped from the station wagon and took the fish from the little boy, and, asking him where his manners were, cuffed him soundly about the ears with it.

I saw that if I was to have any success with my diplomatic mission, I must at once relieve the minds of Bertie's parents by producing the real bride.

"Sugar!" I called, turning towards the station wagon. But it was no longer where it had been. It had started going round and round. I shall always think of Sugar as going round and round, in a car or on a dance floor. There was a kind of place in this driveway where you went round and round. You know the way driveways do, Freddy. They are very confusing sometimes.

So the second time she came round, Sugar hit something. It may have been a chair, or the terrace itself, or a butler—there seemed to be thousands and thousands of butlers about now, sprung from nowhere—and I saw that the traffic cop at White Plains had been right. The station wagon *was* really top heavy.

It skidded, Freddy. Lurched and swayed and staggered, if you know what I mean. For an instant, it seemed as if it were going to tip over. And all those crates and things, which must have jolted loose, flew off the top and landed right onto the terrace. They tumbled over the chairs and coffee cups and everything, and among the guests whom the little mulatto boy had thought were dead people.

They sort of exploded as they crashed, the crates did. I remember ducks and rabbits and chickens bursting out in every direction. There was a good deal of noise, and I have no doubt that Mr and Mrs Duffield and their guests were somewhat startled. Especially as these presents we had brought Mr Duffield became at once mixed with his guests.

One dignified lady, who can only be described as a *grande dame,* lay under a table—it was one of those tables with twisted iron legs—you know, Freddy, sort of scrollwork iron legs that go every which way and make you dizzy to look at them—in a terrible struggle with a fish. It was a mullet, for it seems Caroline was partial to mullets. Freddy, believe it or not, but the mullet appeared to have become alive. It may have been because the table legs twisted in such a queer way that they gave a semblance of motion to everything—I state only what I saw, Freddy—but as the *grande dame* fought the mullet, the mullet appeared to fight back. It was a terrible struggle and was somewhat obscured for me by the dog, who now assisted the *grande dame* and now the mullet.

I was perhaps the only creature there who preserved his poise and equanimity. There was an old gentleman who was trying to get an excited hen out of his beard who used language I should not like to repeat, and a lady who was temporarily wearing several rabbits who also used expressions I have been pretending to myself ever since that I did not hear. But by far the angriest person was a distinguished-looking gentleman who sat on the ground staring at a duck, which stared back at him. They spoke eye to eye, as if fascinated and unable to dissever their regard. This gentleman, I learned later, was a Mr Sloan, a very wealthy man. It seems that he and Mr Duffield were about to fix up some big business deal, which would save the nation's industries and add to Mr Duffield's riches immensely, and now

Mr Sloan was cursing the Duffields to the duck and the duck was complaining bitterly to Mr Sloan.

I thought later that the wrecking of this business deal may have had something to do with making Mr Duffield so unjust and harsh.

"Mr Duffield——" I began.

"You get to hell out of here, young Withersbee," he said. "And take that idiot son of mine with you. And if either one of you ever shows up here again, I'll shoot him!"

"Mr Duffield," I said, "I think you are being very unkind—after we have brought you all these nice presents and everything! I should think you would at least allow me to explain that this evening marks a turning point in Bertie's life."

"You darned well know it does," said Mr Duffield, taking a rabbit from his shirt front and hurling the innocent creature viciously at his son. "Turning point is right—I've talked of disinheriting him before, but now I'm going to do it! The moron!"

I took Sugar by the elbow and thrust her forward.

"Mr Duffield," I said, "you must at least allow me to set you right on one matter—*this* is the lady whom Bertie married. This is Sugar! How anyone can look at this sweet young thing and remain angry is more than I can comprehend."

"Take her away!" cried Mr Duffield. He made an angry gesture.

Sugar's feelings were hurt at this reception—and who can blame her? She had done her part; she had

brought Mr Duffield's son home to him, safely and happily married, only to meet with this bleak ingratitude.

"Good-by, Papa," said Sugar and turned towards
the station wagon. But she spun around swiftly again,
as if with a second thought. "Here's something to remember me by, Papa," she said. I believe I have mentioned that she was a dancer. She stood upon the toes of
one foot, whirled round and round as if to gain momentum, and planted a dainty kick in the middle of Mr
Duffield's shirt front. It was a charming gesture, but he
did not appear to appreciate it. I shall *always* think of
Sugar as whirling round and round and round.

"Papa," said Bertie, as we got back into the car,
where Caroline and the little mulatto boy and the dog
were now cowering, "you are angry now, but you will
get over it and learn to love Sugar, I know."

"Nerts," said Sugar, throwing in the clutch.

"And," said Bertie, as the car started, still address-
ing his father, "it might have been a great deal worse,
Papa. There might have been two of her—and as a
matter of fact there was quite a while when there
seemed to be two of her."

And we drove away in a very dignified manner, per-
mitting Mr Duffield and his guests to have a monopoly
on all the ill nature and impoliteness. Sugar and Bertie
are living in my little flat, Freddy, and she will keep on
with her dancing until the old gentleman relents, or
something. Caroline and the little mulatto boy and the
dog are also in the flat. Caroline says she was hired
away from a good job in Harlem, and intends to fulfill

her contract or know the reason why. There is no room for me. Especially as they all seem to be whirling round and round in there all the time. They were all whirling round and round when I saw them. They were sort of like a floor show.

Sugar told me that Bertie is thinking about beginning to try to look for a job himself. I think family responsibilities are beginning to steady him a little.

I am a little tired myself, Freddy, what with this and that and all the emotional strain I have been through; and I will take a nightcap and curl up on your couch.

EDDIE TAKES A REST

I ASKED Dr Cartwright Carson if he would have a drink. He said yes, and had it in a pitcher. This was necessary, he explained, because the drink he preferred consisted of draught beer, ale and bottled brown stout, mixed in certain proportions, and no glass or stein large enough to hold it, when properly mixed, was in general use.

"This," he said, setting the pitcher down after his first pull, with a long-drawn sigh of contentment, "is one of old Doc Carson's most golden medical discoveries, warranted to alleviate all the ailments of man or beast, and compounded of——"

He interrupted himself for another dive into the pitcher, and then went on:

"I was about to say, compounded of juniper berries, buchu leaves, and the bark of the wild cohosh. But that's only force of habit. It's queer how those old phrases cling to the mind and come tripping off the tongue—that was part of a ballyhoo I used some seasons ago, when I was traveling as an old med. doctor for Siwash Injun Skagrah, nature's own remedy, discovered by the aborigines of Oregon, and now for the first time introduced to the paleface—six bottles for five dollars while we are in your little city, and after our departure a dollar a bottle at your local pharmacy—and with every bottle goes a phial of Dr Carson's Wonder Oil."

Dr Cartwright Carson has done nearly everything. He has been, as indicated, a med. show doctor; he has sold thousands of fountain pens on hundreds of street corners; he has played every part in a Tom show from Simon Legree to the Voice of the Bloodhounds, with the possible exception of Little Eva; he has taken orders for crayon portraits, and sold gallons of indissoluble, indestructible and iridescent pearls; he has employed himself as ringmaster of a flea circus; he has been a mentalist, fortuneteller and spiritualistic medium; he has promoted street carnivals and tree-sitting contests; he has been a rain maker and a crystal gazer; he has shown the heavens through a telescope to multitudes of the curious, imparting meanwhile a lecture on astronomy which might have astonished Professor Einstein. It is to be feared that during the era of Prohibition he had relations with divers citizens who gave no enthusiastic support to the Volstead Act. But he passes lightly over this period of his life.

"In forty years of service to the American people," he said to me, "Dr Cartwright Carson, the old pitchman, has never once gypped nor jammed his public. Old Reliable is his name, and reliable is his nature. Render unto Caesar is his motto, and he always leaves a town clean for the next worker. No business proposition is a good proposition unless it is strictly moral, and never once has honest Doc Carson departed from that maxim."

"Never once?" I inquired. We were sitting in a restaurant on Broadway which is much frequented by ladies and gentlemen who live by their wits, or what have they. I looked about and wondered how many of them could say the same thing.

2

Only once (said old Doc Carson, toying with his second pitcher of the golden medical discovery) did I ever have any remote connection with, or knowledge of, a transaction which might not have stood the scrutiny of a district attorney or the examination of a pastor. I was myself entirely innocent of any wrongful act, and I will relate the tale to you because it is a moral tale. Indeed, it shows that what I have said is true; iniquity does not prosper. Or, at least, not always.

This business proposition was broached to me, oddly enough, in this same hostelry. I was sitting at that very table in the corner there where the blonde lady is endeavoring to make herself agreeable to the swarthy gentleman with the queer face. Poor Mable—she is wasting her time; she does not know that Manny has returned from the races at Saratoga in a condition of well-nigh complete insolvency.

It was before Repeal, and the person who sought me out at yonder table was known to his circle of intimates as Willie Three-Ears. Willie had had a career that was somewhat checkered—and also, I am afraid, occasionally striped. At one time he was a paluka box fighter and had sustained an injury to his right ear which had partially split and thoroughly cauliflowered the same, making it look like two ears. Adding these two right ears to the left ear, you arrived at the sum of three; hence his nickname.

With Willie Three-Ears, when he approached me, were a gentleman known as Dan Handsome—called also Handsome Dan Tulliver—and a person called Lefty, who I have always suspected was a denizen of the underworld. I often wondered if Lefty was not what is called in current slang a gorilla. If he had any other name besides Lefty, I never heard it. Willie and Dan called him that, and that alone.

Willie was renting from me at that time two motor trucks, which I had formerly used in a medicine show. What he did with them was none of my business. He assured me that they were positively *not* used for illegal transportation of liquor. And once when I pointed out to him quite a number of holes in one of them which looked like bullet holes, he told me that those were holes which had been made by woodpeckers on the previous Sunday, when he and Dan Handsome and Lefty had taken some friends for a picnic in the country. "We took some people for a little ride," said Willie Three-Ears; "it was such a nice day."

It was my innocence and good faith which made me attractive to Willie Three-Ears, and also the fact that at that time I had a small house in the Catskills; a modest camp where I used sometimes to retire and commune with nature.

"I could use that house of yours for a few weeks in a little business proposition of mine, Doc," said Willie.

"It is a little business proposition you might want to take a slice of yourself, Doc," said Dan Handsome.

Lefty said nothing. He very seldom spoke, and then his utterance was usually concerned with the most simple material matters, such as food, drink and money. I believe, indeed, that Lefty was not a high type mentally. I have never known a man who consisted so largely of shoulders.

"What do you want with my house?" I asked Willie Three-Ears. It was a cottage with no modern conveniences, situated in rough country amongst the hills, near no road feasible for motorcars; and it would surprise you how nearly inaccessible it was, being only a little more than a hundred miles from New York City. The nearest village more considerable than a crossroads hamlet was a score of miles away. Willie had rented the cottage once before for a period of some months. He had stored goods in it, he said; and had insisted that they were goods of a nature to which the sternest moralist need not object. Otherwise, I should not have let him have it. The motto of Dr Cartwright Carson has always been to keep his hands and his conscience honest and clean. What Willie wanted to store in it this time was a young fellow by the name of Eddie Carter.

"That is a strange idea," I said.

"He is a strange young man," says Willie. "It seems his father is a gentleman by the name of Edward J. Carter, who is very wealthy."

"I've heard of him," I said. Indeed, who has not? His fortune runs into so many figures that it keeps an entire section of the treasury department busy figuring out his income tax and how to get it away from the old gentleman.

"This son Eddie is a great disappointment to Mr Carter," said Willie Three-Ears. "Eddie comes in here a good deal. You may have seen him. He is apt to come in here any time, with a doll or two from some burlesque show, or other attraction of that nature. This Eddie is about twenty-one or twenty-two, and since he left college about a year ago, at the request of the college, he has been getting wilder and wilder and coming in here and other places more and more with these janes and dolls who are not any too good for a young fellow, and his poor old father is getting more and more worried about his future. One of these dolls married him once, and it cost old man Carter $100,000 to get the marriage rubbed out. And another doll got a hundred grand as a reward for giving him up without marrying him. This young man is, I regret to say, a wastrel of the most active kind."

"So what?" says I.

"It occurred to Dan and me," says Willie Three-Ears, "that if we could take this Eddie up to your little house in the Catskills for a few weeks, living there might have a good effect on him—sane, quiet, simple living, you know, Doc, like you read about in the books."

"A kind of a rest cure, you know, Doc," says Dan Handsome.

"Get him in touch with the great throbbing heart of nature, far from the madding crowd?" says I.

"Exactly, Doc," says Willie Three-Ears.

"And it ought to be worth a good deal of money to his father, old Edward J. Carter," says Dan Handsome, "to get Eddie all straightened out and okay again, mentally and physically."

"And morally?" I says, with my usual caution.

"Check, Doc," says Willie Three-Ears.

"Has his father commissioned you to do this?" I asked.

"Oh, no, Doc," says Dan Handsome. "That is going to be one of the nicest things about it all. It will be a complete surprise to old Edward J. Carter. Just think how glad he will be, and how liberally he will reward us, when he gets Eddie home again, all spruced up and reformed and made over into a model citizen!"

"How much had you thought of asking the elder Mr Carter for your services in connection with this rest cure?" I inquired of Willie Three-Ears.

"Mr Carter is very rich indeed," said Willie, "and this Eddie is his only son. We thought that a hundred grand would be about right."

"Suppose that Mr Carter does not agree to that sum?" I suggested.

"I think he will," says Dan Handsome. "Mr Carter is used to paying out a hundred grand every now and then in connection with Eddie, and he may find himself doing it almost automatically. It is a habit he has formed. The sum of a hundred thousand dollars is on his mind where Eddie is concerned. I understand that if you mention Eddie he thinks of a hundred grand, and if you mention a hundred grand he thinks of Eddie."

"In case he does not think quickly enough," says Willie Three-Ears, "it is our idea to extend the rest cure until habit reasserts itself."

"What will the young man himself think of the idea?" I asked.

"We don't expect him to like it very much at the start," said Willie, "for he is not the kind of young man who would appreciate any serious effort made to reform him. So we have decided not to consult him at all in the matter. It will all be a surprise to him, as well as to his father."

"Then," I inquired, "how do you propose to induce Eddie to visit this little camp of mine in the mountains?"

"That will be very simple, Doc," says Willie Three-Ears. "He often leaves this very restaurant, quite late at night, I regret to say, in a state of well-nigh helpless intoxication. What more likely than that he might enter a taxicab driven by Lefty, here? He might even find himself in bed in your little place in the Catskills before he was thoroughly sobered."

"The motive—that of reforming this wild young man—seems entirely moral and quite laudable to me," I said. "But before I rent you my house, Willie, I must be assured that this rest cure which you contemplate for the young man will be a very quiet one indeed."

"Meaning what?" says Willie Three-Ears.

"That you have planned no violent physical exercises for him which could possibly result in his bodily injury," I said. "In fact, that no harm whatever happens to him at my house."

"Oh, of course not!" said Willie Three-Ears and Dan Handsome, in chorus. But I thought that Lefty pulled himself down amongst his shoulders with a slight air of disappointment at this. I could never tell what this Lefty was thinking about; and it is possible that he had long spells when he did not even attempt to think at all.

"We thought the rent for your camp might be a percentage of what Mr Carter gave us in his gratitude for getting Eddie back all straightened out," says Willie.

I devoted a few moments of thought before I answered; with the result that I decided not to rent them the camp at all.

"No, Willie," I said, "I will sell you my camp, cash down; and I do not know, or wish to know, what you do with it. I shall not be a participant in any way in this rest-cure scheme of yours. I admire your motives in wishing to do a kind act for this Eddie and his elderly father; but there are points in it that might be open to serious misconstruction if any meddlesome person with a legal mind became interested.

"We will visit my lawyer's, make over the papers, and I should like the money this afternoon. I wish to take a little trip, so that I will be gone before this rest cure starts; and I shall not return until it is happily finished."

"Those are very hard terms, Doc," said Willie Three-Ears. "We had hoped that you would help finance our plan. The old B. R. is not so very strong just now."

"A good many collections have been made from us lately," said Dan Handsome, "and we will need four or five grand to swing this thing."

But I was firm, and I sold them the house that afternoon and got paid for it.

3

I took a little trip, and I was in Chicago when I saw in the papers that my fears were realized—that Dan's and Willie's efforts on behalf of Edward Carter, Jr, had been misconstrued. In fact, the headlines went so far as to say that he had been kidnaped. There was quite a to-do about it, and a country-wide search was in progress.

According to the public prints, old Edward J. Carter was bearing up bravely under the shock, and his attitude called forth great admiration. He said that the young man was so erratic that he was not thoroughly convinced that he had been kidnaped—he might have gone on a trip without telling anyone. He had done just such things before, and the father had not known where he was until he had received a cablegram from Monte Carlo or Constantinople or Paris urging the immediate despatch of large sums of money. He should not become overly excited, Mr Carter told the reporters, until he heard directly from Eddie himself. It might turn out to be just one of the young fellow's boyish pranks. Eddie was a good boy at heart, he said; but there was no use denying that he had been a bit wild.

Following this, a note from Eddie himself appeared in all the papers, in facsimile, urging his father to pay the ransom, but also stating that he was being well used. Considerable comment was elicited by the fact that this note was mailed from Chicago. I supposed Dan Handsome or Willie Three-Ears had gone to Chicago to mail it—or had it mailed there through some of their business connections. I never knew at any time just what their business was. However, I left Chicago at once and went to Cincinnati, as I did not care to be in the same city from which that note had been mailed, even though the house at which Eddie might be found was not my property.

In Cincinnati I began to make preparations to go on the road again with another medicine show. I regretted exceedingly that I had left at my place in the Catskills my large motorized van, in which I often lived while playing the tank towns, and from the back platform of which I made my pitches and gave my entertainments and sold my remedies. It was especially constructed, after my own design, for my especial needs, and it would cost time and money to get another one.

Weeks passed by, and then more weeks. The Eddie Carter story was still a live story in the papers—front-page news whenever there was any new development—but not front-page news every day. More weeks passed by; two new kidnapings and the shooting of three notorious bandits shoved the Eddie Carter story off the front page entirely. The old gentleman remained calm, for publication at least. And the theory began to gain general credence that it was just one of Eddie's old pranks, and that he would turn up in Cairo or Honolulu, or somewhere, sooner or later, probably married to somebody strange and expensive, from whom his father would have to buy him loose again. Eddie had figured so often in the news since his nineteenth year that people seemed to be unable to take his kidnaping, if he had been kidnaped, as seriously as if he were someone else.

I began to think it might not be imprudent to go back and get my van. I had got a good price for my house— a very good price indeed, for Willie Three-Ears and Dan Handsome had wanted it at once—but I had not sold the van along with it.

I went to New York and took the train to a place called Jelliffe, which is on a lake about eighteen or twenty miles from my house and has some pretensions to being a summer resort. It is not a swell resort by any means, as the vicinity smells a good deal of dried fish at all times. It is surrounded by the cheaper class of amusements and the kind of bungalows you buy at a department store all ready to put together by following a chart with printed instructions. It advertises that it is restricted, but I do not know what it is restricted from; it is certainly not yachting caps, nor girls who go on hikes with knickers and high-heeled shoes, which

will give you a rough general idea of the kind of place
it is.

When I got into Jelliffe I noticed considerable excitement down by the lake, near a summer theater which
had stood tottering on the shore for quite a number of
years. By keeping my eyes and ears open, I learned that
a theatrical troupe—a summer stock company—were
being forcibly evicted from a cottage near the theater.

You know I am keenly sympathetic with troupers of
all varieties, hall show or tent show, and I went over
and got acquainted with them. They had a Ford car
and a trailer and very little else; and it seems they were
not quite certain where they were going. One of them
was a blonde lady in a greenish kind of dress, and she
was Miss Evelyn Lamb, she said, and she had a husband with her by the name of Mr Lamb. Another lady
was very brunette, and you could tell at a glance the
parts she would be cast for. She was Miss Clarice Clay,
and a husband, Mr Clay, was with her also. The dress
she had left was sort of greenish also. The trailer was
quite an affair, and it was fitted up so you could cook in
it and sleep in it, if you could get hold of anything to
cook and were not too much perturbed by the stings of
care and chance insects to sleep. They had hopes, they
said, of eventually getting into touch with something,
though they did not know exactly what; and if they had
a truck which could be used as a platform they would
try their luck going from town to town and giving
shows. They had quite a repertory, which could easily
be cut over to fit such costumes as still remained to

them. So I gave them my blessing and a bottle of
scotch, and they started off along the road quite happy.

I was puzzled as to how to get up to my house—or
rather Willie Three-Ears' house—in the hills. If I
hired a car in Jelliffe to drive me, I might be leading
trouble right to Willie and Dan Handsome, supposing
they were still there. What I wanted was to get to the
house, get my truck and drive away as soon as possible
without seeing anything or knowing anything or making any contact with anybody about whom I might be
questioned later.

About six miles from the house a rough country
road, not much used by cars, left the main asphalted
highway; and the trail from this country road up to
the house in the hills was about a mile long and could
not be called a road at all. If you did not know it was
there, you could not find it, for it was all but concealed
by underbrush and briers—it was just a kind of rocky
scar on the hillside. It was all you wanted to do to get
up there in a powerful truck, such as my van was, or
one of these little flivvers which will go up the side of
a house and hold fast by the stick of the paint—you
wouldn't want to put a high-toned automobile at that
hillside. The house itself was hidden from observation
from any direction by a dip in the hilltop. It was ideal
in every particular for the kind of rest cure which
Willie Three-Ears and Dan Handsome planned for
young Eddie Carter.

I hired a car at a Jelliffe garage and had the driver
drop me near where the country dirt road left the main

highway. When he was out of sight, on his way back to town, I started on my six-mile walk, which was mostly uphill. It was the middle of the afternoon, and hot, when I sat down on the bank of a brook which came splashing and fussing through the hills about a quarter of a mile from the house. I washed my face, took a good long drink of water, and then took my shoes and socks off to cool my feet, which were not used to hitting the grit.

While I was sitting there, I must have dozed off. But presently I heard voices and then somebody moving through the bushes and splashing through the water. And then I caught sight of something up the creek which I at first thought must be a bear with a fish pole. There are bears in that country, and there was a story to the effect that there were trout in that creek, but I never saw any.

"Wot t'hell," says the bear, turning to speak to some-one behind him, "dey ain't no fish in dis crick, boss!"

"You don't know how to cast a fly," said the other person, coming into view. "That's a right-hand fishing rod; what you need is a left-handed fishing rod."

I got a good look at him then; and I recognized him as a young man I had often seen in this restaurant here. It flashed over me that it must be Eddie Carter. He was wading barefoot, with his trousers rolled up—a strong, athletic young fellow, with a shock of red hair and a good-natured grin on his face. He looked the picture of health.

"My fly ain't tryin', boss," said Lefty, disgustedly, for Lefty was the bear.

I wondered about this. Was Eddie Carter in the act of escaping, and was he taking the gorilla, Lefty, with him? Did Dan Handsome and Willie Three-Ears think it prudent to allow their prisoner to ramble the countryside in this fashion? Or was this fishing trip an inspiration of Lefty's own? What was this all about?

Then I saw that Eddie was not unguarded. Swung on holsters, Lefty was carrying, not one, but two, heavy automatic pistols of large caliber.

They had seen me, and paused in the little stream right above where I was sitting, by the time I had remarked this armament. Lefty's mouth dropped open with astonishment, and his head came out from among his shoulders like a turtle's from its shell as he stared at me with popping eyes.

"Hello, Doc," he said, finally. "What you doin' here?"

"I came for my van," I said. "I suppose it's still here?"

"In the shed behind the house," said Lefty. "Truck's oke, but dey ain't no gas."

I turned to Eddie Carter. "I've seen you before," I said. "In Durden's restaurant—often. But I have never seen you looking so well before."

"You're old Doc Carson, the pitchman, aren't you?" he said, holding out a hand which was strong and tanned. "You've been pointed out to me there."

"For a young man with a hundred million people worrying about him, you look pretty cheerful," I said.

"Yes," he grinned. "I'm all right—oke, as Lefty here would put it. It seems that my father isn't one of the hundred million who are worrying."

He looked at me and grinned again.

"Are you," he said, "one of my captors?"

"Not at all," I said. "I know nothing about your abduction or about your captors. I used to own this place, and I came to get a truck I left here when I sold it. I am, in a manner of speaking, a neutral in all this trouble."

"Yes? Let's go up to the house," he said.

On the climb up the hill, Lefty volunteered: "Dan has took his car and went to N'Yawk. Willie's at the house." He added, importantly, "Dan is pulling negotiations." I could understand that it might well be Dan Handsome, rather than Willie Three-Ears, who would do any negotiating which would have to be done. For Willie's appearance, what with his ears and this and that, was not one which inspired confidence at first sight.

"They've left you on guard?" I said.

"With orders," said Eddie Carter, "to shoot to kill, if any attempt is made to escape." He seemed, by his manner, to think this was a huge joke. Then he said to me, with a glance at Lefty, "Dr Carson, I suppose you are thinking you could get quite a reward for giving information about my whereabouts—and about Dan and Willie."

Lefty glowered at me with sudden suspicion. He was a slow-witted creature, and I suppose this was actually the first time the reflection had occurred to him that it was possible I might do such a thing. His hand closed over the butt of one of his automatics.

"Not at all," I said hastily. "I don't even know who you mean by Dan and Willie. I don't even know what Lefty's last name is—or his first one, either, for that matter." Which was no more nor less than the simple truth. And truth and honesty have ever been the slogans of Dr Cartwright Carson, forty years *be*side the family bedside.

4

Willie was at the house, and not in a very good humor. He greeted me politely enough, but it was plain that he was not glad to see me. He was pleasant enough in his manner with Carter, too. But he addressed Lefty as if the man were a dog and began to order him about, telling him to rustle up some grub with rough expressions which I would not repeat to any audience in America. It was plain that this rest cure was getting on Willie's nerves far more than on the patient's, who really seemed to be enjoying it. There were hundreds of New York papers strewn about the living room, and papers from other cities, late papers and papers weeks old. Just a glance at the headlines showed that Willie Three-Ears had been reading about the Eddie Carter case. He looked worried.

As there was no gas on the place, and no way to get

any while Dan was gone with his car, I had to stay all night. I didn't like it, but I stayed. That night, to while away the time, the four of us played poker. It seems there had been a good deal of poker playing while Eddie Carter had been in captivity. They had chips, but until my advent no real money had gone into the game. They had been dividing the ransom money which they were to get from old man Carter into shares and issuing chips to represent the shares. Eddie Carter had issued additional shares on his own responsibility. And the way the thing had turned out, Eddie Carter was so far ahead of the game that when his old man came across with the ransom money, Eddie would get the lion's share of it. That boy was a born poker player.

The little cash game we had that night turned out to his advantage also. And it prolonged itself, as poker has a way of doing, if you've ever noticed. Willie opened up some cases of scotch and rye which happened to be at the house, and we had a meal or two; but at four o'clock the next afternoon we were still playing on the front porch, and still waiting for Dan Handsome to come back with his car, so we could fetch some gas and I could get away with my van. The van itself I had won and lost and won again several times, but Eddie Carter had about all the cash that had been put into the game.

It was a little after four o'clock when we heard a car coming up the hill, making the hullabaloo all cars make when they negotiate that grade. We laid down our cards, and Willie and Eddie Carter got to their feet.

"It must be Dan," said Willie.

"I hope the old man," said Eddie Carter, alluding to his elderly parent in this disrespectful manner, "has softened up. I'd like to see Dan coming back with the cash, for, nice as you boys have been to me, I'm getting kind of tired of it here. And I'd like to have my share of the ransom money that I've won from you fellows playing poker when I leave."

Willie Three-Ears looked pretty glum at that. But he said nothing hasty. What was in his mind, I am sure, was some sharp retort such as, "You poor simp, do you think you are really going to get it?" I've often had my suspicions that Willie Three-Ears was a crook.

It struck me that Eddie Carter did not thoroughly appreciate the danger he might be in, for neither Willie Three-Ears nor Dan Handsome was what I should call a stable and dependable character; and in a fit of anger and disappointment might go very far indeed with something they would regret later. In fact, I wished that I had not even come back for my van. If anything unfortunate were to happen, I did not wish to be in a position where I should have to explain why I could not remember anything about it.

The car which had been scrambling up the hill came out of the bushes. It wasn't Dan Handsome. It was Mr Clay and Miss Clay, and Mr Lamb and Miss Lamb, and their flivver and trailer. They stopped right in front of the porch.

"Hullo, Doc," says Mr Lamb to me, for everybody seems to feel privileged to call me Doc on short acquaintance. And then he says, "Great Snakes, if that isn't Eddie Carter!"

"Hullo, Lamb," says Eddie Carter. And he went on to say, with the air of a young man who is seldom at a loss, "Won't you folks come in and have a drink?"

5

No sooner said than done, and all Willie Three-Ears could find tongue to utter was, "Who the hell are you, and how did you get here?"

The troupers were all staring at Eddie Carter as if they could hardly believe that it was he. But pretty soon Miss Lamb says:

"It was our understanding that our young friend Eddie Carter here had been kidnaped."

"Nothing of the sort," said Willie Three-Ears. "Mr Carter is merely taking a rest cure."

"We have been reading in the papers," said Miss Clay, "that he has been abducted." And she helped herself to a liberal portion of scotch, mingled with a little bit of water.

"We hear he has been shanghaied," said Mr Clay.

"Or snatched, if you want to put it that way," said Mr Lamb. And he also made overt preparations to decorate his internal organs with a highball.

"I tell you, nothing of the sort!" said Willie Three-Ears, trying to look innocent and annoyed at the same time. "He is here to get his health back."

"I am afraid," said Mr Lamb, "that a court of law

might view it as an abduction. It seems he is being hunted for from Labrador to Guadalupe, on the idea that he has been kidnaped."

"Our interest in the matter," said Mr Clay, laying a fond hand upon the bottle, which was beginning to show signs of depletion, "is twofold. In the first place, we are intimate friends of Eddie Carter and have been ever since his college days. We helped him get through more than one tough semester. In the second place, we have recently been evicted from a little cottage, not more than a score of miles from here, which we had been planning to inhabit for the entire season."

"This eviction following the failure of a summer theater," said Mr Lamb. "They almost always fail," he added gloomily.

"So what?" says Willie Three-Ears.

"So we have no place to go," said Mr Lamb.

"We remembered having seen Eddie near here yesterday," said Miss Lamb.

"Well?" says Willie Three-Ears.

"Well," says Miss Lamb, "it occurred to us as we came along the road today, not going anywhere in particular, that we might join Eddie."

"In his captivity," says Miss Clay.

"Be prisoners along with him, you know," said Miss Lamb, pleasantly.

"Share in his adversity, as we have so often shared in his prosperity," says Mr Clay, getting his teeth and tonsils into the line.

"What the hell," says Willie Three-Ears, looking

puzzled, and more annoyed than ever, "what the hell are you getting at? Are you all cuckoo?"

"We are all very fond of Eddie Carter," said Miss Clay. "And if you have a corkscrew, and will open that bottle of rye which I see nestling among the scotch, I will take ginger ale in this one."

"We intend to see Eddie Carter through this trouble he has got himself into," says Miss Lamb, "no matter what the consequences may be."

"If Eddie Carter," says Miss Clay, "is going to be kidnaped, then we are going to be kidnaped, too. Some time, remind me to teach you how to open a bottle without getting cork into its contents."

"Listen——" begins Willie Three-Ears.

"Now, now," says Miss Clay, "don't apologize! It's a thing that might happen to anybody; and it's really of no consequence, anyhow. This eviction which we spoke of took place yesterday directly after breakfast, and it is now dinnertime today. I don't think there is one of us who has had many meals in the interim."

"For my part," said Miss Lamb, "I could do with a substantial portion of ham and eggs."

"I don't suppose," said Mr Clay, gazing at Willie Three-Ears inquiringly, "that you have such a thing as horse-radish in this camp?"

"Mr Clay," said Miss Clay, explaining to Willie Three-Ears, "is very fond of horse-radish with his ham and eggs."

"It's just a notion of mine," says Mr Clay. "Of

course, if you haven't got it, ketchup will do very nicely. I don't want to be troublesome."

Now, I can see by the expression on the face of Willie Three-Ears that he is far beyond his depth mentally and floundering in seas of social experience, so to speak, which he never expected to be asked to navigate. Either these people are cuckoo, or he is cuckoo himself, and he doesn't know which. Both may be true. As for Lefty, he looks dumber than ever, if that is possible. And he fingers his automatic. Willie Three-Ears looks at him and frowns. He is going through agonies of thought. These people are all wise, now, just through his carelessness in letting Lefty take Eddie Carter out fishing, for it was down by the brook that they must have seen him the day before. And a pretty howdy-do that is! And what may come of it? For it would be ridiculous to think you could bump off all those people and get away with it. For I would have to be bumped off, too. And Eddie Carter, likewise. And the veranda would be as full of remains as the stage in the last act of a hall show of the Shakespearean school.

"What the hell!" says Willie Three-Ears.

And just then Dan Handsome arrives, and when he sees our little picnic party comfortably seated with its highballs and what have you, the same phrase rises automatically to his lips. "What the hell!" says Dan Handsome, looking quite surprised and somewhat annoyed.

Willie took him over to one corner of the veranda, and they exchanged news in a low tone of voice. I could see by the looks on their faces that, from their point of view, it was bad news. Willie comes back to our convivial group, and he says, looking daggers at Eddie Carter, "You are free."

"What do you mean by that, Willie?" says Eddie Carter.

"You can go any time, and the sooner the better," says Dan Handsome. "Your old man says he doesn't give a damn if you are kidnaped, and he won't pay a cent to get you back. He don't want you back. He is tired of buying you loose from janes."

"The old so-and-so," says Willie Three-Ears, vindictively.

"Do you mean I'm not kidnaped any more?" says Eddie Carter.

"You are not," he said. And then, with a look at the troupers, he adds, "And you never were. I don't know what you mean by using the expression 'kidnaped.'"

"Listen," says Eddie Carter, "then what becomes of the money I won from you boys playing poker?"

"Beat it!" says Willie. He looked dangerous, and I wished I was away from there. He turned towards the troupers. "And you, too!" he vociferated.

"It doesn't seem right to me," says Mr Lamb, "to turn Eddie loose in the world this way, with no place to go, now that his father has repudiated him. I have a certain sympathy for homeless wanderers, for we have no place to go ourselves."

"Of course," said Mr Clay thoughtfully, "you could be inhospitable and turn Eddie Carter loose on a cold

world, and us, too, but I hope that your better nature
would prevent your doing this before we had all gathered round the festive board, as was suggested some
moments ago. Might I not add that, in the event we
were hospitably entertained, it might have considerable
effect in coloring the story we took to the outside world?
We find our old friend Eddie Carter enjoying an out-
ing at your little place—entirely ignorant of the fact,
as you are yourselves, that there is all this talk about
kidnaping——" He broke off and left the thought with
Willie Three-Ears. I could see by Willie's face that it
was sinking in.

"On the other hand," said Mr Clay, "you could shoot
all of us. But there are quite a number of us, you know."

We all looked around on all of us, and there were—
six, including Eddie Carter himself and me.

"I've got a—— good notion to do it," says Dan
Handsome, who was still out of temper from his inter-
view with old Edward J. Carter. And as for Lefty, he
looked quietly delighted with the idea. For all I know,
it may have been quite in his line. I always try to think
well of people, but try as I will, I cannot think of this
Lefty person as a respectable and honest citizen.

Willie Three-Ears says, with an expression which I
will not repeat, "Stay to dinner, then, and we'll talk it
over." It was not a gracious invitation.

As for me, I did not stay to dinner. I drained enough
gas out of Dan's car to get my truck to the next filling
station and went away from there. Anything of any
sort might break out up there in those hills at any time,

and honest Doc Carson did not wish to occupy a witness chair in any court.

6

"Well?" said I, as the old faker immersed himself in another pitcher of his golden medical discovery.

"Well," said he, "it was six weeks later that I heard what happened next. I ran onto these same troupers in a little town in Connecticut. They were happily losing in another summer theater the money they had got out of Willie Three-Ears and Dan Handsome."

"They got money out of them?"

"Yes—for going away, you know. They stayed a week, with Lefty and Dan and Willie cooking for them and waiting on them. And then Dan and Willie paid them to get rid of them—it was either that, or bump them off, for they knew too much. And there really were too many to bump off. As I said before, iniquity does not prosper—it cost Dan and Willie everything they had."

He suddenly chuckled.

"You're holding back something, Doc," I said.

"Nothing you wouldn't know if you'd read the papers," he said. "Eddie Carter went with the troupe. In fact, he made threatening motions towards uniting himself in matrimony to Miss Lamb—it seems that Mr Lamb wasn't very much of a husband, after all—and it cost old Mr Carter—well, what do you suppose it cost him to stop that?"

"A hundred thousand dollars," I said.

"Exactly. A hundred grand. Dan Handsome was right, psychologically, about the amount. But he failed, somehow, in his approach. They lost their share of it the next season trying to produce plays on Broadway. And my share——" He stopped.

"Your share?" I inquired.

"Yes," he said. "I handled the negotiations myself, looking towards the release of Eddie Carter from the clutches of Miss Lamb. It seems she was something of a harpy, in a nice way." He sighed. "I backed a road show with mine," he said.

GETTING A START IN LIFE

THERE comes a time when every young fellow has got to strike out for himself, but I dilly-dallied around until I was sixteen years old before I became Foot Loose.

The main trouble was old man Humphreys. He had been licking me since I was five years old every time his sciatic rheumatism bothered him or he ate something he couldn't digest or what he read in the papers disagreed with him. He got me from one of these Orphan Asylums in the state of Pennsylvania and moved me to a little town in Illinois we lived on the edge of; and, on account of the Asylum, me being a citizen of one state and residing in another one, I suppose there was no one to check up on how legal these lickings were.

I got very tired of Betty Hartley seeing him lick me so much, because she and I were practically engaged, having split a dime with a cold chisel. The Hartley house was right across the road from the Humphreys farm, and the chances that girl had to see me licked were legion, as the books say.

So one day she says to me she has got her doubts about me being a Hero, or any part of it. She says, "Would John Barrymore or Wallace Beery let themselves be continually licked like that?"

"Yes," I says, making a snappy come-back, "you are

always talking about John Barrymore or Wallace Beery. But I guess Clark Gable is the better actor of all three of them. He is a Hard Guy. If Clark Gable would bounce a fast one off of John Barrymore or Wallace Beery's chin you would soon see which is the better actor of the three!"

Betty is a very romantic girl on account of the reading matter she associates with. The Hartleys have got a whole room full of practically nothing but reading matter—old time reading matter handed down from ancestor to ancestor, Betty says, and from shortly after birth until the age of fourteen she has been eating it up. You know—stuff about Rob Roy and Walter Scott and Scottish Chiefs and Robin Hood and a lot of those racketeers before they invented automatics, and I dipped into a lot of that stuff myself. It ain't reasonable like the Pictures.

Being in love with Betty was no snap; either you had got to be a Hero or you were practically the dirt under her feet. She had the notion maybe I have got royal blood in my veins, or something, for nobody knew who I was as far as parents were concerned. I used to look at my veins careful for symptoms of royal blood, but I could never see anything wrong with them. And I never felt peculiar like a royal family. Just the same, you see things like lost identifications working out in the movies all the time, and it might be true I was somebody royal who had lost his tag. To this day I ain't prepared to say yes or no to that and stick to it. Betty has the idea that my hair has got a natural slick lay-down to it, without any slickum, like this Prince you are always seeing in news reels and Sunday papers.

Often she would rouse my ambition to go out in the world and become a Hero of some sort and conquer all before me and get a start in life and come back and marry her. But how was I going to make a getaway? No railroad comes within miles of that little town of Springville. It is just a few stores and a church and schoolhouse and moving picture palace and a filling station with farms like ours all round about. And if you hitch hike on autos, how do you know where they are going to? But the main thing is, you got to have a little bit of money and some Other Clothes, which I never had.

So I says to Betty: "Yes! Probably Clark Gable or Wallace Beery would bounce a fast one off of old man Humphreys' chin and go out into the world, okay, or any of those Heroes we been reading about. But suppose I was to go too far with it and would contribute some mortal injury to old man Humphreys' frame? What good would being a Hero do me then, if I went to jail for life?"

Betty says in that case she would come every day to my prison and pass a red, red rose through the bars to me, whilst she sung a song like a Heroine we saw in one of these all-color movies with sound effects, song and dialog.

"Okay as far as it goes," I says, "but suppose I was hung?"

It was her idea more likely I would be executed by amputation with an axe, like we read about in Dickens' history of England. Because, she said, if your blood is royal, you are entitled not to be hung; they amputate you like Charles First or a chicken. I says to her:

"Well, I would rather be an Aviator."

So I says to old man Humphreys that same afternoon:

"You can believe it or not, but I would like half a dollar."

You would think from the emotions of his face that I had asked him for forty acres of land and a couple of tractors.

"It would surprise you," I says, "but there's a circus over in the village this afternoon."

"You tell it to come over here, William," he says, "and help you pick and crate up the rest of those apples this afternoon."

He is a skinny old man, and I am so big and stout for sixteen it would surprise you. I had been feeling stouter and stouter all that spring and summer, and wondering if that skinny, stingy old man could lick me, after all, if I didn't let him do it. He bandied further words with me, as follows:

"And if you sneak away from here and crawl under that tent, all the lickings I have given you in years past won't be a circumstance to the one you will get this time. Circus! Huh! Circus!"

So I sneaked away and crawled under the tent as usual. Coming home late in the afternoon, I was wondering what would a man's chances be if he was to run off and join one? Would it be a Stepping Stone? Could a guy get into aviation that way? Or into the movies? Well, believe it or not, the Secret Service had always held out a kind of fascination to me, too; also being a radio announcer. But the movies would be a sure thing, because for two years I had been going over into the woods lot and practicing stunts. Well, also, maybe I would go West and punch cattle. Also, you could learn to throw your voice and be a ventriloquizer. And sometimes I felt the light heavyweight championship of the world would be a good thing to grab onto whilst I was still young. Believe me or not, I was getting fed up with farm work. At the same time a young fellow has always got to ask himself, is this going to be a Stepping Stone, or ain't it?

So old man Humphreys was waiting for me with a strap out in front of the house. Betty climbed down out of an apple tree in her orchard and came on over. The way she looked at me she was saying to herself either I am going to turn out to be a Hero, or else I ain't.

"What are you going to do with that strap?" I said, exactly like I did not know. And if I had had a cigaret I would have lighted it, and I would have liked to have had on one of these suits of Tuxedo evening clothes whilst I was saying that. "What," I handed him, "are you going to do with that strap?"

He bandied words with me as follows:

"You take off your coat and I'll show you, you . . ."

I leave out several words on account of Betty being

present during their utterance, as they were not the class of words she should have heard.

"Suppose," I says, wishing I could be flicking the ashes off that cigaret if I had one, "suppose that after all I was to fail to take off that coat?"

He came at me whirling that strap, and the next thing anybody knew, believe it or not, he was on the ground and I had him by one ear and some whiskers and was kind of jouncing his head into the gravel.

He bandied further words that should not have been heard by Betty, who never had much experience with language except she got it out of books, and made a big claim that I was probably killing him, on account of his sciatica and this and that. And Betty says, "Make him yield, Willie, make him yield!"

At first I was kind of pleased, and I says to him:

"Probably I could have done this any time the last couple of months, Uncle Henry!"

For, when I was a child, he had always taught me to call him Uncle Henry when I felt affectionate towards him.

He replied with language as see above, and worse. Ordinary men should not have heard it, let alone ladies or preachers. And he followed that up with words even hard guys would think a couple of times before uttering.

So I began to get scared. If he was that mad he would probably lay me out cold with a piece of iron if I let him up; he would be practically a maniac. At the same time I was afraid that if I kept on jouncing his head it would kind of go to pieces right there on the road. The more language he used the more I jounced, for I was excited. It was a great crisis in my life, and anything I did was bound to be wrong, and Betty gave me no advice except the most romantic kind, jumping up and down and yelling to make him yield.

Ma Humphreys, which is his wife, came out and stood on the front porch with a palm-leaf fan. She is quite a fat lady and very calm and soothing at times, and she says:

"Why, Willie, what on earth are you doing with your Uncle Henry?"

"I am resigning from this farm," I says.

Ma Humphreys says not to dissect him completely. I knew that lots of times she must have wished something like this would happen to him, but she has always been too plump and dignified to do it herself; so now she just fans herself and lets well enough alone. But I am wondering will his head hold out until his mad streak leaves him and I dare to let him up—for it would be a pretty poor start in life to get hung for this! I says to Betty:

"Look at the trouble you got me into, swelling me up to be a Hero! It is just like a girl!"

She began to cry, and I saw I must have said the wrong thing somehow. And just then a strong hand gripped me and saved me from destruction.

And that was the first time I ever got acquainted with Tobey Bailey. He stopped his big van, which I had not even heard coming along the road, and he yanked me off old man Humphreys, with the following dialog:

"You young wildcat! Do you want to kill him?"

"No, sir," I says, "I been trying to persuade him he ought to quit licking me."

He says he thinks I got him almost persuaded, like the old song says. And then he remarks he never saw anyone look more so, not from Greenland's icy mountains to India's coral strands, see the hymn books.

So Ma Humphreys brings a basin of water and some Liniment for Man and Beast and gets him onto the porch and starts to fix him up, and I saw what was painted all down one side of Tobey Bailey's van. The van was the biggest of any kind I ever saw anywhere, and the letters were enormous and red, as follows:

TOBEY BAILEY'S TRAVELING EMPORIUM.
HIGHEST PRICES FOR RAGS, OLD IRON, COPPER.
HAIR BOBBED, AUTOS REPAIRED.
I BUY, SELL, EXCHANGE, REPAIR, INSTALL,
RADIO SETS.
TINWARE, CUTLERY, WRENCHES, BUTTONS, TOOLS.
ORDERS TAKEN FOR HIGH GRADE TOMBSTONES.
SEWING MACHINES MENDED, BOUGHT, SOLD, TRADED.
FLOWER SEEDS, SAXOPHONES, HAIR NETS.
TRY TOBEY'S CORN AND BUNION CURE.
JOKE BOOKS, COOK BOOKS, SONG HITS, HYMN BOOKS.
I LOCATE WATER OR YOUR MONEY BACK.
TRY TOBEY'S LINIMENT FOR MAN AND BEAST.
TEETH PULLED, BOUGHT, SOLD, EXCHANGED.

"Well, Horace," says Tobey Bailey to me, as I finished reading these signs, "you seem interested in my business. More interested than I would suppose a young criminal to be in trade."

"His name is not Horace, but Willie," said Betty, who had hold of my arm. "He is not a criminal, either." And I could not keep her from going on and saying that more than likely I had royal blood in my veins.

Tobey Bailey says I look more to him like a revolutionary than a royalty.

"Here," he says, with quite a gesture of his arms, "here the embattled farmer stood, and fired the shot heard round the world, Ralph Waldorf Emerson."

He was full of quotations like that and the authors he quoted them from. He was a big man, about forty-five, very good-natured, and you could not always tell when he was joshing you. He wanted to know if old man Humphreys' blood was royal, too; he could see considerable of it being sponged off of him. And had the Lion and the Unicorn been fighting for the Crown, Mother Goose?

Betty began to tell him the story of my life, all mixed up with her romantic notions, and how I was looking for a start in life, and was going to come back and marry her, and I went around to the other side of the van. The signs on that side bandied the following information:

TOBEY BAILEY'S TRAVELING EMPORIUM.
KNIVES GROUND, CLOCKS FIXED, LOCKS MENDED,
SAWS FILED.
I AM TOBEY THE RAIN MAKER.
PUMPS DOCTORED. FLUES CLEANED. BALDNESS
CURED.
BEST PRICES FOR EGGS AND BUTTER.
SHAVING SOAP, RAZOR BLADES, PHRENOLOGY,
WASHING POWDER.
PHONOGRAPHS REPAIRED. RECORDS. NEEDLES.
TOBEY TELLS WHAT CHEMICALS YOUR SOIL NEEDS.
ORDERS TAKEN FOR BOOK OF ETIQUETTE.
PATTERNS, ASTROLOGY, BIRD SEED, ELECTRIC BELTS.
TOBEY SLAYS ALL INSECT PESTS.
MY TRAINED PIG TELLS YOUR FORTUNE.

When I had read them he came around to my side
and said, "Well, William the Conqueror, I understand
you are now At Liberty."

I said, "But where is the Trained Pig that tells fortunes?"

"Gone," he says, "along with his caretaker." And
then he sighed and remarked, "All, all are gone, the
old familiar faces, Charles Lamb."

He says the pig's name was Lord Chesterfield, and
him and a young fellow who was working for Tobey
disappeared at the same time, and he's got the idea one
of them stole the other one, it matters little which. If it
has come to acute hunger by this time, he says, he is
afraid cannibalism has been put across ere this, which,

he says, it would be in either case. So I asked him if Lord Chesterfield could really tell fortunes.

"I could teach even you to do that," he says. "Lesson you to peer into the crystal sphere and pluck the secrets from the heart of life." He smiled at me and said, "Tobey Bailey!" Meaning that one he was quoting from himself.

He traded and bartered and repaired through little towns like ours and the farming country between, and made county fairs and street carnivals besides, and could do all sorts of stunts and be all kinds of things, more even than was on his van, and he lived in the van and often camped by some crick over night. And he needed an assistant who could take care of the van and drive it when he wanted to sleep or read, and who could make himself useful in a thousand little ways, he says. I told him the great question with me would be: Is it a Stepping Stone?

"Yes," he says, "I see what you mean—men should rise on stepping stones of their dead selves to higher things, Lord Alfred Tennyson. But where do you want to step to, William?"

"Aviation," I says, "for one thing. Or else," I says, putting all my cards on the table, "possibly moving pictures with sound effects and dialog, if you were going in the direction of Hollywood."

"I go in all directions," he says. "The wind bloweth where it listeth. If you come with me you might wind up in Hollywood or you might wind up in Quebec. Or you might never wind up at all." He says to look at himself—he has been going somewhere always, and he has never wound up anywhere yet, and probably never will now. "Let us then," he says, "be up and doing, with a heart for any fate, Henry Wordsworth Longfellow."

So I thought I would go and say good-by to poor old Uncle Henry and forgive him, but he says for me to get to a place I will not write out of there. And Ma Humphreys says, "Willie, you better sleep over to the Hartleys' tonight; he has got one of those tempers on him."

When I turned back to the van, Betty was leaning up against it, and she was crying. Tobey Bailey was saying to her, "There, there, honey, don't take on so! I won't take him along with me if you're going to feel so bad about it!"

"Oh, I will never see you again!" Betty says to me.

"Betty," I says, "in just a few months I will fly back in an airplane and take you away with me. Or else maybe you will soon see me in the pictures or something. Or maybe hear me announcing artists and events on the radio. So don't bawl this way—because I am now getting the start in life we have been wishing for. You are spoiling everything by the way you are acting! It is just like a girl!"

"Oh," she says, "you don't care about me—you are only thinking about yourself!"

I saw I had said the entirely wrong thing again. All of a sudden she started to scramble into the van, and she says, "I am going, too!"

"No, no, honey, you can't do that," says Tobey Bailey. And he lifted her down into the dusty road again. He says to me, "William, maybe you'd better stay here."

"I got no place to stay, now," I says, thinking of old man Humphreys.

And we all three stood there and said nothing for a little while, and from the way Tobey Bailey looked at Betty and at me you could see he was thinking thoughts along with both of us. For it came to me all of a sudden like this was the end of the World, somehow. And how mean it had been of me a minute ago to think only of my own start in life, and not of Betty! For I could see it was like the end of the world to Betty, too. We had both been talking for months and months about how, some time, I would leave here and get my start in life, and when we had talked it was always full of joyfulness and hope. But now it wasn't like that. It was like the end of the World. Maybe we had not completely believed I would leave when we had talked about my leaving. Maybe that was it. But here, all of a sudden, right in the middle of the road, here it was! Not talk about it, but the real leaving! It had come onto us kind of quick.

Tobey Bailey looks from her to me and says the maid who binds her warrior's sash the while her pain dissembles can feel upon her drooping lash a teardrop where it trembles, Lord Byron or Somebody, and if I am going to go, I better make it short, he has found in his experience that is the best way.

I climbed up on the seat, and Betty just stood.

"Well, good-by," I said.

"Good-by," she says.

That was all either of us could say. She looked awful little there in the road. I knew I ought to have got down and kissed her good-by. I never had kissed her but three or four times. But I ought to have kissed her then. But I was afraid to on account of not wanting to leave maybe, and then later if I did not leave I knew I would blame it on her. So I says to her again:

"Well, good-by."

And she says again, "Good-by."

Then there wasn't anything to keep me. For I did not have any clothes, much, except what I had on, and no money, and nothing else. So Tobey, he started his engine, and then he let in the clutch, and we started in first speed.

Betty threw herself into a patch of dusty clover by the side of the road and kicked her heels and tried not to cry, and I started to get down from the seat. But Tobey Bailey grabbed my shoulder. "No," he says; "short and quick is the way; don't even look back— never look back!"

But I did, as the truck made more speed, and when we got to the curve in the road she had got to her knees and was waving her arm at me, and I waved back, and then we went around the bend. Nobody said anything till about five miles from there Tobey got down and traded a Swede a bottle of tonic—which he says is made from buchu leaves, juniper berries and the bark of the wild cohosh—for a chicken. About three miles further on we made camp by the side of a crick, and I says:

"Mr Bailey, do you suppose it would eat into her mind, and keep on eating and eating and eating, till probably in the end she would find a place in some crick like this deep enough to drown herself in?"

He says, taking it by and large, he must have seen a thousand cricks like this in all the years he's been going around the country, man and boy, and never but once, he says, did he ever see a girl drowned in one of them. And she was a much older girl than Betty, he says, and she did not drown herself because some fellow she was sweethearts with had gone away, she drowned herself because a fellow she was married to had come back. So he says he eats a good many chickens in his wandering life, and it would be nice if I learnt his way of cooking them, which he showed me then, and he gives me something to smear on myself guaranteed to keep off mosquitoes, which it did not entirely do. And in the morning he says do I possess the great gift of snoring and worrying at the same time? I asked him Why?

"Because," he says, "if you snore only when you sleep, you must have slept the whole night through." For he says I snored from dewey eve till break of dawn, John Milton. And he's glad I did not put in the night wakeful and worrying about Betty.

"You don't know how romantic she is, Mr Bailey," I says. And a good deal of the time for a week he put in trying to cheer me up, for it would come again and again to my mind I was practically a murderer leaving her so sudden, and she had probably pined away by this time. He says to quit mourning and moaning all the time, for I reminded him of the moaning of doves in innumerable elm trees, Lord Alfred Tennyson. And couldn't I laugh a little and dance like a sunbeam on the lea?

So we pitched at a county fair and he introduced me to a good many artists of all kinds, which he had known them here and there and everywheres. There was Dr Cartwright Carson, the old pitchman, who just now was selling indestructible, indissoluble and iridiscent pearls that could not be told from the native product of the deep-sea bivalve, the doctor says. And Mazie, the World's Greatest Escape Artist, who could get out of anything, Tobey says, and had often done it, including the bonds of frequent matrimony. And the Siwash Injun Skagrah outfit, with real Injuns. And Isis, the Fortune Teller: Tobey says she was the Greatest Mentalist ever saw the jack inside a customer's leather pocket book. And a man named Professor Something was living off the earnings of a pack of Trained Fleas, and Tobey says turn about is fair play, for he suspects when times ain't so good the fleas live off of the Professor. And some old pals of Tobey's, pitchmen, who he called Mister Tripes and Mister Keister, was showing you new planets and things with a telescope. And a Bearded Lady in a side show whose real name was Tim Mulcahey. And a fat lady whose husband complained all the time of the expense she was to him, on account of her eating so much it took all his profits he made showing her; and it kept him slaving like a dog. I never had any idea there was so many different kinds of artists on earth and so many different sciences as Tobey Bailey introduced me to. And there was a lady in a faded green dress who charmed a snake. He was a kind of feeble old snake; he had been charmed so much he had lost his interest and ambition. Tobey Bailey says that snake had seen so many different Charmers come and go in the twenty years he's known him that that snake has got to be a woman hater, and he wished he could get that snake to write the story of his life. And plenty of rides and games and concessions. And horse races and auto races. And a flag pole sitter and some amateur tree sitters. And an Aviator on the fair grounds would take you up for a Merely Nominal Sum. Well, believe it or not, I was glad I handed in my resignation to old man Humphreys.

So one day Tobey Bailey looks at me, and he says, "Moderation is the jewel of life, Ralph Waldorf Emerson. Or maybe you don't believe that, Willie?"

"I believe every word Mr Emerson ever said," I bandied back at him, not wishing any part of an argument.

"Do you consider a Hot Dog Sandwich every five minutes during the last twenty-four hours to be moderation?" says Tobey Bailey. "To say nothing of the mustard you been eating on them and the ginger ale you been washing them down with."

"I always understood a growing boy needs a lot of food," I says.

"All that mustard is more likely to stunt your growth," he comes back at me. "What is her name?"

Her name was Myrtle. Her Dad ran the Hot Dog stand right next to our pitch, and the reason I've been eating so many Hot Dogs is so I could get a good chance to talk to her. And the reason I want to talk to her is she looks like Betty, in my estimation.

"Yes, there's a great resemblance," says Tobey. "Barring the fact that Myrtle is an inch or two taller, and has black eyes and dark hair, while Betty has yellow hair and blue eyes—and that Betty is a plump child and Myrtle is skinny—they are practically twin sisters."

"I hadn't noticed all that so much," I says. "They both kind of reminded me of Greta Garbo, and that is what made them remind me of each other."

"Huh!" says Tobey Bailey. "And what do you and Myrtle talk about?"

There's no use trying to conceal anything from Tobey Bailey; so I says, "We talk about how well I like mustard on my Hot Dogs."

Because when I could not think of anything more to say to her I would say, "I would like a little more mustard, please."

And she would come right back with, "The bottle is right there on the counter, help yourself."

So that way we got up quite a joke between us. She had very nice white teeth when she laughed. She would laugh and say I liked a lot of mustard. And I would laugh and say, Yes, I was getting to be quite a mustard eater! But I was careful we should not go too far with it, either, for if she was to fall in love with me it would not be completely honorable on account of Betty.

I would have liked to talk to her about Betty, but the nearest we ever got to that was once I said to her, "You remind me of Greta Garbo." And she laughed and came right back, after a minute or two, with, "That is nice, but I think you are jollying me!" So in a minute or two I asked her for some more mustard.

So I explained to Tobey Bailey, and he looked pretty serious, and he says, not contented with breaking one fond heart I've got the ambition to break two of them, I am a regular Donn Jooan, he don't see how I can sleep nights, one foot on shore and one at sea, men were deceivers ever, The Bard of Avon.

And that night I had Remorse. I woke up screaming with it, a kind of a nightmare of remorse, it settled right in the Pitt of my Being. The next morning I did not want any Hot Dogs for breakfast as usual. I was sad. I could not bear to think of talking to Myrtle and eating. I would not have cared if there was no more mustard in the world. I says to myself: "What a traitor I been to Betty, poor girl, pining away there in that little town of Springville, and me out in the world having a gay time, with bottle after bottle of ginger ale! I have not even sent her a Post Card! I will send her one of this town we are in at once, showing the new high school building they got here, poor girl!" So I says to Tobey Bailey:

"Do you think their new Elks Club here is a better looking building than their new high school?"

Because always, hereafter, as long as I lived, I would never be false to Betty again, if only she got over this time without suicide and never found out about Myrtle. And I would always give her the best there was! There was some big Iron Elks in front of the Elks Club, pretty nifty looking.

It was quite a city, that town, and quite a fair, too. Tobey Bailey won quite a sum of money for me and him on a horse race on account of knowing the Jockey quite well who rode the horse everybody expected would win. But this Jockey made quite a percentage, Tobey says, by the other horse winning.

I got me some Other Clothes over in town at once. It was a great grief to me Betty could not see me in them. It made me sadder than ever to think the way I been treating her. I would not have risked getting mustard on them for anything.

So a Hard Guy was bumped off that night near the Fair Grounds. He was in some gang mix-up or something. Quite a lot of us were standing and looking at the Corps, which had just been found beside the road near the entrance of the Fair Grounds. And a young fellow says to me that business was more dangerous than Aviation. His name was Joe, and he was the Mechanic for the Aviator who was taking them up for a Nominal Sum.

Joe and me became quite Fast Friends right away, and I sort of let Mr Bailey look out for himself for some hours, and admired how Joe knew all about that airplane. Not a part of that engine he did not know, not a nut or a bolt anywheres on that machine. He has never been Up alone yet, but he felt confident he could, and some of these days when Mr Jamieson is not looking he will take me Up, he says.

But at night remorse came onto me once more. We both slept in the Van, there was lots of room and two neat bunks. By the head of my bunk hanging on a wire hanger was my new Clothes, very striped and nifty, and new shoes under the bunk. A little breeze came through the Van, and when the Clothes would swing I would think of Betty, poor girl, and how she had never seen me in them, and all that night my heart was breaking. I had been too busy with Aviation to send her that card with the New Elks Club on it, poor girl! If she killed herself I would be to blame! I had more nightmares, which proved it could not have been merely mustard and ginger ale the other time, as Tobey Bailey had dropped a broad hint. And when the clothes would swing, my nightmare would say to me that was Betty swinging there, she was a very romantic girl and had hung herself on account of me.

So I must have been quite dissipated looking for lack of sleep when I got up in the morning. I put on my new Clothes, and a necktie guaranteed was the real nifty up-to-date goods the college boys were wearing this year, and a hat with a band as see above, and my new shoes with the laces as see above, and the socks was guaranteed similar. And I had walked once or twice past Myrtle's dad's Hot Dog stand, thinking of Betty and praying in my mind she had not croaked herself.

But I did not eat anything; my heart was broken in spite of my swell get-up. I was sad. I just walked around the Fair Grounds that way, sad and dissipated looking, with those Clothes on, and I wondered how many of the people I passed by would know those Clothes concealed a broken Heart! I smiled very bitterly to myself, from time to time, to think little they knew or cared! One corner of a new silk handkerchief was sticking out of my top pocket of my new coat, and I had some of this slickum stuff on my hair. Well, I said, internal, you Merrymakers do not know! You think I am one of you! Ha! Ha! Look closer, and you will see! Or maybe no one will ever see! A doom walks through your midst! Go on in your joy, but a Stranger is walking through your midst who sees how Hollow it all is! I hope no other girl will be attracted to her Destruction!

So after while I walked over to the Flying Field part of the Fair Grounds, and there was Joe in his khaki suit, and Mr Jamieson was not taking anybody up that moment. Joe was explaining about the airplane to a Girl, and her parents were standing by listening and smiling, and you could have knocked me over with a feather, but the parents was Mister and Missis Hartley!

Who else could the Girl be but Betty? She was

dressed in pink, and I sailed up to her and I almost kissed her right there before everybody, I was so over-joyed. She turned around from where she was giggling with Joe, and she says:

"Oh, hello!"

I came right back at her; I says, "Hello!"

Mister Hartley says, "Why, Betty, from the way you act one would think you didn't know Willie!"

Betty says, "Why, Papa, of course I know Willie Humphreys! He used to live at Springville."

Used to live! And this was the girl I had thought most probably had hung herself! And it was only two weeks ago! Well, believe it or not—and if so could you scarcely blame me for it—but my soul turned to ashes in my mouth right then and there! More especial as she says to Joe:

"That is a boy I used to know a long time ago. He used to live a little ways off from our house. I used to know him when we were kids."

I never been so disappointed in my life. My heart was broken, and me thinking all the time probably she had drowned herself in the crick or something! And all the untold agonies I had suffered, and all the Remorse, night after night! And you would have thought it was a thousand years ago and she scarcely knew me except as a Passing Acquaintance. My Pride came to my Res-cue, for after all you got to be a Hard Guy sometimes.

So I took my handkerchief out of my top pocket of my coat, and I brushed some Imaginary dust off of my coat cuff, and I says very polite to Mister Hartley:

"Yes, I remember Springville quite well! It is an interesting little town. I remember Betty too. How she has been growing! She used to be quite a Reader in years past. If there is a Mister Humphreys still there, tell him some nice message for me; I used to know him pretty well at one time. Tell Missis Humphreys I have gone in for Aviation."

So I went over to the Hot Dog stand. I says to Myrtle, "I will have a bottle of ginger ale, the Canada extry dry kind, and a Hot Dog, with plenty of Mustard onto it."

She says, "The mustard is right by your elbow, help yourself. Don't get any of it on that swell new suit!"

I says, "Yeah? A lot you would care about that, Myrtle, wouldn't you? You Girls are all alike!"

I almost choked when I ate it. My heart is still broken. I took Myrtle to the Pictures last night and told her all about it. And Tobey Bailey he says one nail drives out another, Lord Robert Browning, and next week we are going to a Street Carnival. But the great question in my mind is, had I ought to go along with him, or get better acquainted with Mr Jamieson the Aviator? He might be a Stepping Stone!

ENTIRELY LOGICAL

I WISH to consult you not only as an attorney—said Mr Carbury Waters to his lawyer—but as a friend of some years' standing. My wife informed me some hours ago that she intends to sue me for divorce. I want you to defend me; and so I shall tell you, without reservation or equivocation, everything that has happened since eight o'clock last evening, daylight-saving time. You shall be the judge as to whether I deserve all the opprobrium and persecution to which I have been subjected.

No, thank you, I will not have a drink; and if you think that I need a drink to brace me up, that shows that you do not appreciate the fact that I am perfectly poised mentally and in full possession of all my faculties. Moreover, I am contemplating giving up all alcoholic beverages permanently. Although I am, as you may readily see, quite all right now, there was a brief period some hours ago when I conjecture that I was partially under the influence of something that is known as Savannah Artillery Punch. I do not know anything about Savannah, or the kind of artillery they have there, or why this artillery should be brought here to New York and trained upon people who do not know anything about Savannah. That is a point upon which I wish to consult you later, as my attorney, for if there is a good deal of that going on, it is a thing that public-spirited citizens must get together and put a stop to.

No, thank you, I will not take off my mackintosh. If I appear to you to be perspiring, it is not because I am too warm. You have a keen legal mind, and you know what is meant by mental agony. If it is true that I am perspiring it is probably because of mental agony. That is my deduction, from what has happened to me, and you must agree that it is an absolutely logical deduction.

More than that, if I took off my mackintosh you would see at once that I am wearing evening clothes. And you might draw some entirely erroneous conclusion from the fact that I have appeared at your office at two o'clock in the afternoon in evening dress. But if you will listen patiently you will understand that it is quite logical that I should now be wearing evening dress. During the last hour I have been gratuitously insulted by a stranger because of my evening clothes. The man stood next to me in a subway car and repeatedly made a noise in my very face which resembled the noises that are made by these little wooden birds that pop out of clocks. Hundreds and thousands of other persons who were in the subway train applauded him for this undignified and irrational behavior. I shall leave it to your keen legal mind whether it was not quite logical on my part to ask this man why he did not go back into his clock where the works are. It has been my observation that if they do not go back after they have made that noise twelve times, there must be something the matter with the clock; but I counted very carefully, and he far exceeded twelve in the number of his birdlike exclamations. He said to me that no man of any spirit would take words like that without resenting them, and he pushed me, leaving the marks of his soiled fingers on my shirt front. So I got out of the subway and bought this mackintosh to cover my evening clothes.

I ask you to tell me frankly, as a keen legal mind and almost the only friend I have left in the world, whether the purchase of this mackintosh was not the action of an entirely logical person in full command of all his faculties. I dwell upon this rationality in myself because so many other persons have been acting in such a strange manner that I wish you to understand that it is they who have been illogical, and not myself. I see a fountain pen on your desk. Will you make a note, please? Make a note to the effect that through all my sufferings I have been dignified. Thank you.

I am a ruined man. Not only is my wife going to divorce me, but I am ruined financially. I am ruined socially. A very promising career has drawn to a sudden and unfortunate close, just at the hour when the great prize of years of endeavor seemed to be within my grasp. Tomorrow my picture will be in the tabloid newspapers. Please make a note, for I want you to have all the important facts. Make a note of the fact that none of this has been my fault.

It was at nine o'clock this morning—I am precise about the hour, for I remember perfectly looking at my wrist watch—that I began to perceive that people were inclined to treat me a little queerly. I said to Bowers, who has been, as you know, my valet for many years:

"Bowers, do you know how they make Savannah Artillery Punch?"

"Yes, Mr Waters, I do," he said, "and I will tell you all about it later. But first you had better come out of the boat."

"Out of what boat?" I asked him. And I still think it was an entirely logical question.

"The rowboat you are in," said Bowers.

"So it is your notion that I am in a rowboat, is it?" I asked. I wish to state that this was a merely rhetorical question. From the instant that Bowers had mentioned a boat I had known perfectly well that it was a rowboat that I was in. But I thought I had better test him out. Bowers has always been truthful, and I trust him implicitly. Still, it has been my observation that even the best of servants will get careless and neglectful at times about minor matters. And Bowers can be very opinionated. I decided to check up on him and see how much he really knew about this boat he was talking about so glibly.

"You think I am in a rowboat, do you?"

"Yes, Mr Waters," he said, "you are in a rowboat."

I determined to lead him on. "Since you are so dogmatic about it," I said, "maybe you will give me your idea as to where this rowboat that you are talking about is located?"

"In the lake," said Bowers.

"Naturally, the lake," I replied. "Necessarily a lake or pond. I know that it cannot be in a river or stream of any sort, or it would be drifting downstream. And this boat you claim I am in is not drifting." I give you this as an example of my mental acumen even then—at nine o'clock this morning, an hour when, I will admit, I had yet not fully emerged from the influence of this subtle concoction brought up here by artillerymen from Savannah; and as a proof of my logicality throughout.

"What lake—what particular lake—do you claim this rowboat is in?" I went on, continuing to apply the acid test to Bowers. You have a keen legal mind, and you know all about acid tests and third degrees. "There are lakes and lakes, Bowers."

"This lake is in Central Park," said Bowers.

I had no objection to that, and I let it pass without contradicting him. Bowers has been with me since long before I was married, as you know yourself, and I humor him about a good many things.

"Very well, Bowers," I said to him, "for the sake of argument we will say this is Central Park. But what then?"

"If you will come out of the boat," he said, "and come home with me, I will tell you what then."

I have a most perfect recollection of every word I have uttered since exactly nine o'clock this morning, and of the motives behind each word I have uttered, and of every word that has been said to me. Please make a note. You must have all the facts before we can go into court. The fact is that I have at all times a most excellent memory, and since nine o'clock this morning my memory has been almost superhuman. Jot down the fact that my memory is almost superhuman. Thank you.

I remember quite clearly thinking that I had better check up on Bowers a little more thoroughly before I humored him by leaving the boat. I have a keenly logical mind, and I wish always to get the motives of other people quite clear before I act. So I said to him:

"I will not leave the boat, Bowers, until you tell me how Savannah Artillery Punch is made."

"Well, Mr Waters," he said, "you begin by taking a lot of strong, cold tea."

"Tea?" I said. "I thought so! Tea has never agreed with me. Are there cucumbers in it?"

I wanted to see if he really knew. I had a vague feeling that I had come into contact, not so very long before, with cucumbers. I am a tolerant person, with very few prejudices, but I would like to have you jot down here and now that I hate cucumbers.

"You probably had the cucumbers in the salad at dinner," said Bowers. "But don't you think you had better come home with me right away, Mr Waters? People are beginning to come into the park, and they will begin to notice us before long. We don't want a crowd around, wondering about your evening dress, and maybe a policeman."

"What else does it have in it besides tea and cucumbers?" I asked him. For I do not to this moment accept the absurd hypothesis that I would eat cucumbers in a salad.

"Rum," said Bowers. "You put a big lump of ice in the punch bowl, and then you pour tea over it. Then you add rum. Then you put in the brandy. . . . Mr Waters, I see a policeman over on the other side of the pond, talking to the man who is opening up that refreshment stand. I wish you would row the boat ashore and come home with me before they notice you and come over here."

"Are there fruit juices in it, and little bits of fruit like sliced oranges and pineapples floating about?" I asked him.

"Yes, sir," he said. "You put in Apollinaris water and then you stir it and sweeten it to taste. And then you let it get very cold. Just before you are ready to drink it you pour in the champagne. Now, Mr Waters, won't you come home with me before those people come over to this side of the lake? They have noticed us."

"It is a very mild drink, is it not?" I asked him. Again, the question was merely a test question, in consonance with my determination to see if Bowers really knew what he was gossiping about or was merely being pleasantly conversational. I have always allowed Bowers a great many liberties, and sometimes he will gabble inconsequentially on and can scarcely be checked. "Gabble" is the only word for it. Please observe my motive in this cross-examination of Bowers.

"I have heard that it is scarcely to be distinguished from a mild fruit cup, sir," said Bowers, "while it is being partaken of. And that leads many persons who are not acquainted with its properties to drink more and more of it, indefinitely. Then, sir, there comes a reckoning—it comes quite suddenly, sir, and gentlemen who have partaken too freely, if I may use the expression, pass out of the picture. I have heard of instances where they did not recover their faculties completely for more than thirty hours, sir. . . . And now, Mr Waters, won't you take hold of the oars and row up to this rock where I am sitting, and let me help you ashore? Just one little push with the oars, Mr Waters! More and more people are gathering on the other side of the pond and pointing at you."

"Probably you have formed an opinion as to where I partook of this fiendishly deceitful drink," I said, "and when?" And I added that he should be cautious in his answer, for I was checking up on him. If he had tried to influence me to believe that I had drunk it in Savannah and had rowed to New York in the boat in a species of prolonged coma, I should have lost confidence in him at once. The thing is patently impossible, and I dismissed it from my own mind the very moment it occurred to me, thus affording another proof of the logicality of my mental processes.

"Yes, sir," he said. "You went to dinner with Mr Jenkins last night—his last bachelor dinner before his wedding to Mrs Purdy today. The wedding is at high noon, Mr Waters, and if I am to get you to it we must go home at once and you must have some strong coffee and some rest."

"Of course I went to Mr Jenkins' dinner," I said, very much relieved to find that Bowers had not tried to lie to me. I can remember very clearly being amused at his absurd idea that I could rest after drinking strong coffee. He should have known that it always makes me sleepless. "Savannah," I added, "was settled by pirates, was it not, Bowers?"

"Yes, Mr Waters," said Bowers, "undoubtedly it was."

"Well, then," I said, "maybe you will tell me what you are doing wandering about Central Park at this ungodly hour of the morning?"

"I have been looking everywhere for you, Mr Waters, since you did not come home at six o'clock this morning."

"Why six?" I said. "I don't quite see that. Why pick out six? There are several other hours this morning when I did not come home."

"It was at six, sir, that Mrs Waters and her mother, having expected you all night, became very much alarmed over your continued absence and sent me out to search. I must say that I had very little expectation of finding you, and I wandered here and there at random, hesitating to inform the police and not really being greatly alarmed myself, sir. But half an hour ago, walking about the park, I was guided to this pond by the sound of your voice. You were singing, sir."

I did not believe any of this for a moment. It was obvious that he was concealing something from me. But

I let it pass. And in another moment I caught Bowers in a patent prevarication.

"What was I singing?" I said.

"You were singing the words of a lullaby, Mr Waters, but I did not recognize the tune. It interested me, sir, even before I recognized that the voice was yours, because it was the first time I had ever heard a lullaby sung so very loudly, as if it were a drinking song."

"Let us see what sort of memory you have—what were the words?" I said.

"The words, Mr Waters, were, 'Hush, my babe! Lie still and slumber.' "

I saw that it was time to discharge the man. Even an old retainer cannot expect to be forgiven for such impertinences. I paddled the boat up to the shore beside the rock on which he was sitting, and stepped out of it, and was about to tell him that, much as it grieved me, I must give him notice, when he suddenly caught at his forehead with his hands and appeared to stagger. I recall perfectly the expression which Bowers used, and his manner. I thought his evident emotion excessive at the time, and I still think so.

"For the love of heaven, Mr Waters," he said, "a baby! A baby!"

Please make a note. I was not astonished. I perceived a small child asleep in the bottom of the boat, but I did not for one moment lose my equilibrium. Make a note to the effect that I remained calm and retained complete control of all my faculties. Indeed, I endeavored

to quiet and soothe Bowers himself. I thought it best
to attempt this by taking his mind off the subject, and
so I said to him:

"I have a great piece of news for you, Bowers! Mr
Jenkins announced at the dinner last night that I was
to become a full partner in his banking business, and
first vice-president."

You know yourself what a conservative private banking business Jenkins runs, and how well I have deserved
the promotion. I thought that Bowers would rejoice
with me in my great good fortune and cease to stare at
the baby in the boat and jabber incoherently. But I was
mistaken.

"Mr Waters," he said—and I remember his exact
words—"don't you see there is a baby in that boat?"

"Of course," I said, "it is easy enough to see that
there is a baby in the boat. Like Moses in the rushes.
And that reminds me. The man that mixed that punch
at Mr Jenkins' party last night was a Mr Rush—Mr
William Rush. He had learned it, he said, in Savannah."

But Bowers persisted in his selfish emotionalism.
"Mr Waters," he said, "for heaven's sake, push that
boat out into the water and run away from here before
the policeman arrives and sees the baby!"

Please make a note. I did not run. I have at all times
a keen psychological instinct, and it told me now that
the way to invite pursuit and capture was to run. The
policeman, I noted, was approaching us on the winding
asphalt path which skirts the lake. About twenty per-

sons—I wish to be precise, and so I will say somewhere between twenty and twenty-five persons—had followed him, but the policeman had told them to stay back.

"Mr Jenkins," I said to Bowers, "made a neat and witty little talk, and said some very nice things about me."

"Where did you get it, Mr Waters?" said Bowers, with a very illogical agitation.

"I told you," I said, "that this man Rush made it. I didn't notice what he was putting in it. It tasted quite mild."

"I mean the baby," he said.

"Well, what is your opinion?" I said. "You have opinions about everything, and I let you have them because you are an old servant. Where do you think I got it?"

"Oh, heavens!" said Bowers. This was his exact expression.

"Pick it out of the boat," I said, "and make it quit sucking its thumb. Don't you know that if they suck their thumbs they ruin the shape of their mouths? And if it is a girl and she finds out that you are responsible for letting her ruin the shape of her mouth, she will never forgive you when she grows up. It makes the teeth project."

"Oh, heavens!" said Bowers. And again I am careful to report his words accurately. But he stepped to the boat and picked up the child and took its thumb out of its mouth as I had directed. It waked up and began to cry. I took it from Bowers at once. And just then the policeman came up and looked at me and at the baby and wanted to know if soup and fish was a new kind of uniform for nurses. The crowd that had been following him had stopped a hundred yards or so away—or let us say a hundred and ten yards—and I noticed that another policeman was keeping them there.

"You mean a new kind of food, don't you?" I said. His mention of the uniform is still incomprehensible to me.

"What I mean is," he said, getting red in the face, "that I have been watching you for fifteen minutes, and I want to know why the deuce a man in a full-dress suit is rowing a baby about the lake in Central Park at nine o'clock in the morning."

"Ask Bowers there," I said; "he's probably got some theory about that. He has theories about everything."

"Whose baby is it?" the policeman asked.

"It's mine," I said. "Don't you see whose finger it is nursing? Be a little logical, can't you, and a little more courteous?" It had quit crying when it got hold of my finger.

He turned to Bowers and stared at him for a minute without saying anything, and I am glad to say for Bowers that the stare seemed to do away with the rest of his silly emotionalism.

"Well," said the officer to Bowers finally, "does the baby really belong to that nut?"

"Yes, sir," said Bowers. "But he isn't a nut. He's my employer. He came home from an all-night party a little the worse for wear, as you can see for yourself, and said he was going to take the baby out for an airing. He got out with it before the Missis could stop him, and I followed on to see that nothing happened to either of them. It's quite all right, officer. He's going home now."

"It sounds phony to me," said the officer. He took out a little notebook. "Where do you live?"

Bowers gave him the address of the apartment house on Park Avenue where I reside, and he turned to me.

"What's your name?"

"Rush," I said—"Moses Rush." Now, as you know very well, that is not my name. But an inspiration had suddenly come to me. I felt certain that Mrs Waters would wish to adopt this baby. It has been one of the disappointments of our married life that we have had no children. And I knew that if I gave my real name to this officer it would be very easy for people who might wish to take the baby away from Mrs Waters to trace its whereabouts. I think very quickly in emergencies, and very logically.

"I am," I added, "from Savannah, Georgia." This, as you with your keen legal mind will readily perceive, was also calculated to deceive the officer as to my identity. I could not bear the thought of my wife becoming attached to this baby and then having to give it up.

"Who are you?" he said.

"Don't be stupid, officer," I replied. "I have just told you that I am Moses Rush and that I came originally from Savannah, Georgia."

"I mean, what's your business?" he said.

"I am in the artillery business," I replied.

"Artillery business?" he said stupidly.

"Mr Rush manufactures cannon," said Bowers.

"Oh," said the officer. I am giving you his exact expression. He wrote down the information.

"Now," said Bowers, "Mr Rush and I are going home. Mrs Rush will be worried nearly to death."

"I'm going with you," said the policeman.

"I'll look after Mr Rush and little Moses," said Bowers. "It's not necessary for you to go with us."

"The hell it ain't," said the policeman. "I'll come along and see if you really live there."

Then he called to the other policeman, who was making the crowd stay back, "All right, Mike! I'll take care of this."

So we started out through the park with the baby still nursing my finger. But in one of the walks—to be precise, the one that passes by the zoo and is hidden by trees and shrubs from the street and from the other walks—Bowers stopped beneath a bridge and drew the officer aside.

And in a moment the officer had left us, and Bowers and the baby and I were going on alone. Bowers explained that they both belonged to the same lodge.

"And now, Mr Waters," he said, "we'll take a taxi on Fifth Avenue; I'll drop you at home and take this baby to a police station and say I found him in the subway."

I do not think it is possible to begin a child's education too young. I can remember the lasting impression

that seals made on me at a very early age, and what
this communication with nature has meant to me all
my life since. I said to Bowers, "I am going to show
Moses the seals in the zoo before I take him to my
wife."

"For the love of heaven, Mr Waters," said Bowers,
giving way to his facile emotionalism once more, "let
me get you under cover first and then get rid of this
baby!"

"You don't understand," I said. "Try and follow my
reasoning, Bowers. I have been out very late. Mrs
Waters has been anxious. She has been grieved. Her
mother has been anxious. Perhaps both of them are
a bit irritated. But when I arrive with Moses they will
forgive me for being late. Mrs Waters will appreciate
my thoughtfulness in bringing her this baby to adopt.
We have wanted children. She will be beside herself
with joy."

"I doubt it, Mr Waters—I seriously doubt it," said
Bowers. "But at any rate, let us show him the seals
some other time, Mr Waters."

I let him have his way about that, for the baby was
beginning to cry again. And it came to me very suddenly that I did not wish, myself, to see seals bobbing
about in a tank. I must be frank with you. Make a note,
please, that I am concealing nothing. The fact is that
seals bobbing in a tank would remind me of ice and
pieces of fruit bobbing about in a punch bowl, and I
never wanted to see a punch bowl again.

"Is Savannah on an island?" I asked Bowers as we

got into a taxicab. "With water jiggling all around it?"

"No, Mr Waters," said Bowers. "What made you think that?"

"I know it is an island; it seceded," I said. And I still have a distinct impression that Savannah once seceded from the state of Georgia. But I let him have his way about it. One gets tired of the eternal argumentative stubbornness of these spoiled old servants such as Bowers. "It seceded when the state of Georgia went dry, long before the war." And I added, "In spite of that, these Savannah artillerymen are not going to have their way with little Moses. I am going to bring him up a teetotaler."

Moses impressed me as a very agreeable baby when not crying, and I realized that it was a perfectly logical thing for the child to cry. He was undoubtedly hungry. I must describe him more in detail for you, so you will understand my affection for him was entirely rational. He was a baby with blue eyes and three very sharp small teeth. The inside of his mouth was quite strikingly red, and there was a good deal of pink ribbon about him. His shoes were blue, and on the whole it was a most engaging color scheme which he presented. I think I liked him more than most babies because he seemed to be very fond of me; swallowing, with every evidence of relish, a large pearl which I had worn as a stud in my dress shirts for some time, and thanking me for it afterward with the most grateful gurgles. I easily foiled Bowers' clumsy attempts to take him from me in order to carry him to a police station, and pres-

ently the taxi was gone, and in another instant Moses
and I were advancing with outstretched arms down the
vast extent of my own living room to greet my wife and
her mother.

"Here is Moses," I said happily, turning the baby
with his head up so that he would make a better first
impression.

I was totally unprepared for what happened. Both
women screamed. I am not exaggerating in the slightest degree.

"Whose baby is that?" said my wife, shrinking back
from us.

"Mine," I said. And I was about to add "And yours,"
and explain to her that she and I were to adopt it,
when she interrupted me with another outcry.

It will probably be incredible to you, but I must tell
you the facts, and the fact is that my wife from that
moment seemed to conceive a definite distaste for little
Moses. I can only characterize her manner as hysteri-
cal and violent. Will you please make a note to the effect
that women are illogical?

I make no pretense of reporting in detail the events
of the next few moments. I admit freely that they confused me to a certain extent. This was at ten o'clock
this morning; and at ten o'clock this morning, while my
logical faculties were working splendidly, they were
not working so swiftly as they are at the present moment. I mean to say, they were accurate and trustworthy if given time, but they were still somewhat
slowed up because of the machinations of this man

Rush, who had brought up from Georgia to Mr Jenkins' party the reason why these artillerymen are always seceding.

Mrs Waters called me a brute.

This grieved me. I had tried to be kind and thoughtful. I had, in splendid sympathy with her baffled maternal instinct, brought this child to her to adopt. And she called me a brute.

Her mother called me a cold-blooded murderer.

I made an endeavor to get their minds away from this train of thought, which I saw at once was going to end by making them unhappy. I said:

"Did you ever know a man by the name of Rush? From Savannah, Georgia? Because it was in this man's very presence that Mr Jenkins told me last night that I was to be junior partner henceforth, and first vice-president."

The storm that this announcement called forth is impossible to describe.

Gradually, as I listened and endeavored to hush little Moses, whom I was joggling on my knee, I realized that my wife and her mother were accusing me of having been unfaithful to my marital vows for years. It was their theory that I had successfully concealed my infidelity until a callous and brutish inebriety had made me boastful of it, and that I was now deliberately flaunting in their faces this baby, whom they believed to be the illegitimate offspring of myself and some other woman.

"I brought him to you to adopt," I told my wife,

and was about to go on to explain that, as far as I knew, he had no parents whatever, when I was again interrupted.

They informed me that the crowning insult was my suggestion that my wife adopt him.

"Who is the other woman?" my wife demanded.

I was aware at this point that Bowers was in the room. I reflected that he had got me into this mess by not taking the baby to the police station as he had originally intended, and it was only logical and fair that he should get me out of it.

"Bowers," I said to him, "you have been silent for some time. No doubt you have been developing some theory as to the parenthood of this child. All that I ask is that you tell the truth, the whole truth, and nothing but the truth."

"Yes, Mr Waters, I will," he said. And he turned to my wife.

"Mrs Waters," he said, "you are, if I may be permitted to say so, quite wrong in accusing Mr Waters of improper conduct. Quite the contrary to that, ma'am, he has played the part of a hero. He has saved this child, at the risk of his own life, from a fate worse than death."

"Thank you, Bowers," I said. "Go on."

"What fate?" asked my wife.

Bowers was silent for a moment, controlling his emotions.

"Tell her, Bowers," I said. "Speak up. You have nothing to conceal."

"Yes, speak up, Bowers," said my wife's mother. "What fate?"

"From the moving pictures, ma'am," said Bowers. "A movie director was coaxing him from his humble parents to make a child actor of him, when Mr Waters interfered. A terrible fight ensued, but Mr Waters was victorious."

Mrs Waters' mother sniffed. I have never been attracted toward elderly ladies who sniff. "Where are these humble parents now?" she inquired.

"They live on Fifth Avenue," I said. "I fought practically all night. This movie bandit's name was Rush. One of the Savannah Rushes."

Mrs Waters intimated that she thought Bowers' story a falsehood. I was hurt.

"You will be telling me next," I said, "that I was not at Mr Jenkins' party last night, and that I am not first vice-president and junior partner."

I began to remember some of the circumstances which Bowers had narrated—dimly, I confess. I admit that there was a period that was almost a blank to me, owing to the deceitful character of this mixture that was invented by the Savannah pirates. I deduced that it was during this almost blank period that my battle and my rescue of the child had taken place. Make a note, please, of the unimpeachable logicality of this deduction. But I began to remember more and more about it.

"This moving-picture man," I said, "was disguised as the chauffeur of a taxicab. He hit me in the eye."

You can see for yourself that one of my eyes is discolored and swollen. You have a keen legal mind, and I ask you whether this eye is not in itself evidence of the battle which Bowers had described and which I now recalled perfectly. Believe me or not, it was not accepted as evidence.

"Moses," I said to the child, which I was dandling on my knees, "you believe in me, don't you?"

The question was merely rhetorical. I had no notion that the child could speak.

But to the surprise of Bowers and myself he threw his arms about my neck, as if in answer to my appeal for sympathy, and kicking me affectionately in the stomach, remarked:

"Daddy!"

The utterance was unfortunate. Mrs Waters and her mother insisted that it was conclusive proof that I had been leading a double life.

It was then that Mrs Waters announced her determination to divorce me.

I arose with a great deal of dignity, and Moses and I went into my own room, followed by Bowers.

"Mr Waters," said Bowers, "I shall draw your bath now, and then you must get to bed. Do it to please me, sir, won't you?"

I was astonished at the callousness of the man. Here was this helpless infant, unfed for hours; and all Bowers could think of was his own selfish pleasures.

"Bowers," I said, "get some warm milk and a nursing bottle at once."

"Where will I find a nursing bottle, sir?" the man asked. I permitted myself a touch of sarcasm.

"At a boot-and-shoe shop, of course," I said. "You wouldn't think of going to a drugstore, would you?" Please make a note that this is a further proof of the logicality of my own actions and of the illogical state of mind of others with whom I have been in contact today.

While Bowers was absent, Moses consumed two more shirt studs and a bit of the cold cream which I commonly use after shaving. This interested me, for I deduced at once that he was an original child. My observation of my sister's children, who are quite ordinary children, has led me to believe that the usual child, if given pearl studs to play with, immediately pokes them up his nose. But Moses, without hesitation, put his studs into his mouth. Evidently a child with a touch of genius.

Bowers returned at exactly 10:20 o'clock with the nursing bottle full of warm milk, and in a state of reprehensible excitement. He said he had gone to the drugstore around the corner on Madison Avenue for the nursing bottle and that he had found the whole neighborhood there buzzing with excitement. Over the drugstore were a number of flats, and it appeared that the wife of a bookkeeper living in one of these flats had sent her young colored nursemaid to the street with the baby at about eight o'clock that morning to give him an early airing. The colored nursemaid had left the child in its carriage on the sidewalk while she went inside the drugstore to partake of her first ice-cream soda of the day. Upon her return to the street, after this material self-indulgence, she had discovered the baby and carriage gone. Not only she but the parents and the neighborhood were very greatly agitated.

It was Bowers' theory that I had passed this drugstore on my way home at about eight o'clock in the morning and had wheeled the baby over to the park, where he had found me an hour later.

Your keen legal mind will tell you at once that this hypothesis of Bowers was, on the face of it, quite absurd. My observations of young Moses had shown me that there was a touch of genius and originality in him which showed conclusively that he could not be a child of an ordinary bookkeeper. In the second place, the story did not tally at all with the story Bowers had told to my wife and her mother. Either Bowers was lying to me now or else he had lied to my wife and her mother. But as I dimly remembered the struggle of the night before and my battle with Rush, the moving-picture magnate, I was convinced that this was the true explanation of Moses' appearance in my life.

I saw that I could no longer trust Bowers. It was evident that he had been tampered with. I began to see that a conspiracy was forming against me. But I did not choose to reveal everything that was in my mind, since this man had now exposed himself as an enemy of Moses and myself.

So I said to him—rather cleverly, I thought—to

throw him off the track, "You see how badly Moses needed his milk, don't you, Bowers?"

Indeed, he was taking it from the bottle with all the aplomb of an old hand at that sort of thing. He added three half-pint bottles of it to the pearl studs and cold cream which he had consumed, and I said to myself that a child with a digestion like that would go far. For it is an indisputable fact that a sound physical organization is necessary to success in life, even though one may have all the characteristics of a genius. Your logical mind will enable you to follow me.

Moses went to sleep after his third bottle, and as he lay there and I looked at him I meditated upon his future. It was apparent that, since my wife intended to divorce me, he had no future with her and me. My experience in the last hour with women had made me determine never to marry one of them again. The logical thing to do was to find Moses as good a home as possible with the right kind of people, and as soon as possible.

I knew I must act quickly, and I knew I must act secretly, for I felt, with the uncanny psychological instinct which I possess, that invisible forces were closing in upon Moses and myself. I determined to let him have his comfortable sleep out, however, before starting out to search for the right kind of home for him. He seemed so peaceful and contented that it would have been a pity to waken him.

It was, therefore, exactly noon when I made my secret exit with him from the apartment house, descending with him to the basement in the dumb-waiter, so as not to attract impertinent attention. From the basement we made our way through the court into the street and up Park Avenue.

I took a taxi and directed the driver to go very slowly, keeping near the curb, so that I could look out the window and scan the faces of the people passing along the sidewalk. I am an infallible judge of character. One glance at a man and I know instantly whether he would be kind to animals or a suitable parent for children. This holds true with regard to women. We had driven up and down Park Avenue several times, between 57th Street and 96th Street, and a half-hour had been consumed in this manner without my having discovered a suitable foster father for young Moses, when I suddenly realized that we were passing a church.

I stopped the taxi, giving the driver a generous pourboire, and the taxi disappeared as if by magic.

I had had a sudden inspiration, and I acted upon it with the directness and expedition which you have perceived in my character. It occurred to me that I would leave Moses in the lobby of the church. From time immemorial infants have been left in the lobbies or upon the steps of churches, have been adopted by church bodies and have attained distinction.

As I entered the lobby of the church I noticed a number of persons were hastening into the auditorium. Then I heard music. Moses also heard music. He began to chant in response to it, and I perceived he was an artistic child, responsive to rhythm. The rhythm of this music I myself found to be very engaging. It was, in fact, a march.

As I entered the aisle of the church I perceived that it was Mendelssohn's Wedding March. I have always preferred this to the other wedding march—I have forgotten its name, but your keen legal mind will tell you the one I mean. I began to march solemnly, but with a sort of joy, down the aisle toward an ecclesiastical gentleman whom I saw standing at the altar. I was gratified to perceive that Moses continued to chant in unison with the music and that he also swayed himself and his arms and legs in harmony with the rhythm.

Presently I was pleased to note in my progress down the aisle that I was in the midst of friends. And an instant later I perceived Mrs Purdy coming one way toward the altar, surrounded by bridesmaids in step with the music, and then I saw that my dear friend Jenkins was coming from another direction toward the altar, also stepping in harmony with the music.

It struck me at once that there would be no kinder or more thoughtful thing than to give Moses into the custody of Mr Jenkins and Mrs Purdy, who were about to be married. Mr Jenkins I had always thought of, until this morning, as one of the kindest and most benevolent of men. He is about fifty-five years old, and he has been a bachelor since birth. A great many persons have insinuated from time to time that his bachelor existence was a very gay one indeed, but I have never credited these reports.

As I marched down the aisle toward him with Moses

in my arms, I thought of the fine things that he had done for me in the many years past, including his crowning kindness of making me his junior partner and vice-president of his very dignified and conservative banking business. Here was my chance to do something striking for him as a public expression of my sincere gratitude and affection. Perhaps you will think I was sentimental. Perhaps I was sentimental. I admit that my heart was very warm toward him and Mrs Purdy at that moment. They have been engaged for some years. I already considered Moses as their beloved adopted child, and tears swam in my eyes as I thought of the good fortune in store for all three of them.

"Here, Jenkins," I said as I reached the altar, extending Moses toward him—"here, Jenkins, is your baby."

I have never been more deceived in a man's character! He looked upon Moses and myself with a stare of aversion—positive aversion! Moses felt it as well as I. Moses turned from Mr Jenkins and stretched out his arms toward Mrs Purdy.

"Mamma," he said. "Mamma, take!"

But there was no reciprocative welcome from Mrs Purdy. She repudiated Moses with a swoon, thus creating what she should have known would be an awkward social situation. I handed him to the preacher.

I will not attempt to describe what followed, beyond saying to you that the irrational actions on the part of other people which I have noticed all day reached their height in that church during the next ten minutes. I distinctly remember prayers and curses.

But the things that hurt me worst were the remarks made by Mr Jenkins, who, only the night before, had announced at his own dinner party that he intended to make me vice-president and junior partner of his private banking business. I will not repeat them. It would seem incredible to you. He turned upon me like a serpent. Of all the hundreds of people in that church, I was perhaps the only one who retained his dignity.

And in a dignified manner I left it. There is very little more to tell. It can all be summarized by saying I came down here to put my case into your hands.

And now I am very tired. If you do not mind, I will curl up under your desk and take a nap while you are getting your notes in shape, for I want to go into court with this case as soon as possible.

THE RIVERCLIFF GOLF KILLINGS

OR WHY PROFESSOR WADDEMS NEVER BROKE A HUNDRED

I AM telling this story to the public just as I told it in the grand jury room; the district attorney having given me a carbon copy of my sworn testimony.

THE CASE OF DOC GREEN

QUESTION: Professor Waddems, when did you first notice that Dr Green seemed to harbor animosity towards you?

ANSWER: It was when we got to the second hole.

QUESTION: Professor, you may go ahead and tell the jury about it in your own words.

ANSWER: Yes, sir. The situation was this: My third shot lay in the sand in the shallow bunker—an easy pitch with a niblick to within a foot or two of the pin, for anyone who understands the theory of niblick play as well as I do. I had the hole in five, practically.

"Professor," said Doc Green, with whom I was play-ing——

QUESTION: This was Dr James T. Green, the eminent surgeon, was it not?

ANSWER: Yes, sir. Dr Green, with whom I was playing,

217

remarked, "You are all wrong about Freud. Psycho-analysis is the greatest discovery of the age."

"Nonsense! Nonsense! Nonsense!" I replied. "Don't be a fool, Doc! I'll show you where Freud is all wrong, in a minute."

And I lifted the ball with an explosion shot to a spot eighteen inches from the pin, and holed out with an easy putt.

"Five," I said and marked it on my card.

"You mean eight," said Doc Green.

"Three into the bunker, four onto the green, and one putt—five," I said.

"You took four strokes in the bunker, Professor," he said. "Every time you said 'Nonsense' you made a swipe at the ball with your niblick."

"Great Godfrey," I said, "you don't mean to say you are going to count those gestures I made to illustrate my argument as *golf strokes?* Just mere gestures! And you know very well I have never delivered a lecture in twenty-five years without gestures like that!"

"You moved your ball an inch or two with your club at every gesture," he said.

QUESTION: Had you really done so, Professor? Remember, you are on oath.

ANSWER: I do not remember. In any case, the point is immaterial. They were merely gestures.

QUESTION: Did you take an eight, or insist on a five?

ANSWER: I took an eight. I gave in. Gentlemen, I am a good-natured person. Too good-natured. Calm and philosophical; unruffled and patient. My philosophy never leaves me. I took an eight.

(*Sensation in the grand jury room.*)

QUESTION: Will you tell something of your past life, Professor Waddems—who you are and what your life-work has been, and how you acquired the calmness you speak of?

ANSWER: For nearly twenty-five years I lectured on philosophy and psychology in various universities. Since I retired and took up golf it has been my habit to look at all the events and tendencies in the world's news from the standpoint of the philosopher.

QUESTION: Has this helped you in your golf?

ANSWER: Yes, sir. My philosophical and logical training and my specialization in psychology, combined with my natural calmness and patience, have made me the great golfer that I really am.

QUESTION: Have you ever received a square deal, Professor, throughout any eighteen holes of golf?

ANSWER: No, sir. Not once! Not once during the five years since I took the game up at the Rivercliff Country Club.

QUESTION: Have you ever broken a hundred, Professor Waddems?

ANSWER: No, sir. I would have, again and again, except that my opponents, and other persons playing matches on the course, and the very forces of nature themselves are always against me at critical moments. Even the bullfrogs at the three water holes treat me impertinently.

QUESTION: Bullfrogs? You said the bullfrogs, Professor?

ANSWER: Yes, sir. They have been trained by the caddies to treat me impertinently.

QUESTION: What sort of treatment have you received in the locker room?

ANSWER: The worst possible. In the case under consideration, I may say that I took an eight on the second hole, instead of insisting on a five, because I knew the sort of thing Dr Green would say in the locker room after the match—I knew the scene he would make, and what the comments of my so-called friends would be. Whenever I do get down to a hundred an attempt is made to discredit me in the locker room.

QUESTION: Well, you took an eight on the second hole. What happened at the third hole?

ANSWER: Well, sir, I teed up for my drive, and just as I did so, Doc Green made a slighting remark about the League of Nations. "I think it is a good thing we kept out of it," he said.

QUESTION: What were your reactions?

ANSWER: A person of intelligence could only have one kind of reaction, sir. The remark was silly, narrow-minded, provincial, boneheaded, crass and ignorant. It was all the more criminal because Dr Green knew quite well what I think of the League of Nations. The League of Nations was my idea. I thought about it even before the late President Wilson did, and talked about it and wrote about it and lectured about it in the university.

QUESTION: So that you consider Dr Green's motives in mentioning it when you were about to drive——

ANSWER: The worst possible, sir. They could only come from a black heart at such a time.

QUESTION: Did you lose your temper, Professor?

ANSWER: No, sir! No, sir! No, sir! I *never* lose my temper! Not on any provocation. I said to myself, Be calm! Be philosophical! He's trying to get me excited! Remember what he'll say in the locker room afterwards! Be calm! Show him, show him, show him! Show him he can't get my goat.

QUESTION: Then you drove?

ANSWER: I addressed the ball the second time, sir. And I was about to drive when he said, with a sneer, "You must excuse me, Professor. I forgot that you invented the League of Nations."

QUESTION: Did you become violent, then, Professor?

ANSWER: No, sir! No, sir! I never become violent! I never——

QUESTION: Can you moderate your voice somewhat, Professor?

ANSWER: Yes, sir. I was explaining that I never become violent. I had every right to become violent. Any person less calm and philosophical would have become violent. Doc Green to criticize the League of Nations! The ass! Absurd! Preposterous! Silly! Abhorrent! Criminal! What the world wants is peace! Philosophic calm! The fool! Couldn't he understand that!

QUESTION: Aren't you departing, Professor, from the

events of the 29th of last September at the Rivercliff golf course? What did you do next?

ANSWER: I drove.

QUESTION: Successfully?

ANSWER: It was a good drive, but the wind caught it, and it went out of bounds.

QUESTION: What did Dr Green do then?

ANSWER: He grinned. A crass bonehead capable of sneering at the progress of the human race would sneer at a time like that.

QUESTION: But you kept your temper?

ANSWER: All my years of training as a philosopher came to my aid.

QUESTION: Go on, Professor.

ANSWER: I took my midiron from my bag and looked at it.

QUESTION: Well, go on, Professor. What did you think when you looked at it?

ANSWER: I do not remember, sir.

QUESTION: Come, come, Professor! You are under oath, you know. Did you think what a dent it would make in his skull?

ANSWER: Yes, sir. I remember now. I remember wondering if it would not do his brain good to be shaken up a little.

QUESTION: Did you strike him, then?

ANSWER: No, sir. I knew what they'd say in the locker room. They'd say that I lost my temper over a mere game. They would not understand that I had been jarring up his brain for his own good, in the hope of making him understand about the League of Nations. They'd say I was irritated. I know the things people always say.

QUESTION: Was there no other motive for not hitting him?

ANSWER: I don't remember.

QUESTION: Professor Waddems, again I call your attention to the fact that you are under oath. What was your other motive?

ANSWER: Oh yes, now I recall it. I reflected that if I hit him they might make me add another stroke to my score. People are always getting up the flimsiest excuses to make me add another stroke. And then accusing me of impatience if I do not acquiesce in their unfairness. I am never impatient or irritable!

QUESTION: Did you ever break a club on the course, Professor?

ANSWER: I don't remember.

QUESTION: Did you not break a mashie on the Rivercliff course last week, Professor Waddems? Reflect before you answer.

ANSWER: I either gave it away or broke it, I don't remember which.

QUESTION: Come, come, don't you remember that you broke it against a tree?

ANSWER: Oh, I think I know what you mean. But it was not through temper or irritation.

QUESTION: Tell the jury about it.

ANSWER: Well, gentlemen, I had a mashie that had a loose head on it, and I don't know how it got into my bag. My ball lay behind a sapling, and I tried to play it out from behind the tree and missed it entirely. And then I noticed I had this old mashie, which should have been gotten rid of long ago. The club had never been any good. The blade was laid back at the wrong angle. I decided that the time had come to get rid of it once and for all. So I hit it a little tap against the tree, and the head fell off. I threw the pieces over into the bushes.

QUESTION: Did you swear, Professor?

ANSWER: I don't remember. But the injustice of this incident was that my opponent insisted on counting it as a stroke and adding it to my score—my judicial, deliberate destruction of this old mashie. I never get a square deal.

QUESTION: Return to Dr James T. Green, Professor. You are now at the third hole, and the wind has just carried your ball out of bounds.

ANSWER: Well, I didn't hit him when he sneered. I carried the ball within bounds.

"Shooting three," I said calmly. I topped the ball. Gentlemen, I have seen Walter Hagen top the ball the same way.

"Too bad, Professor," said Doc Green. He said it hypocritically. I knew it was hypocrisy. He was secretly gratified that I had topped the ball. He knew I knew it.

QUESTION: What were your emotions at this further insult, Professor?

ANSWER: I pitied him. I thought how inferior he was to

me intellectually, and I pitied him. I addressed the ball again. "I pity him," I murmured. "Pity, pity, pity, pity, pity!"

He overheard me. "Your pity has cost you five more strokes," he said.

"I was merely gesticulating," I said.

QUESTION: Did the ball move? Remember, you are under oath, and you have waived immunity.

ANSWER: If the ball moved, it was because a strong breeze had sprung up.

QUESTION: Go on.

ANSWER: I laid the ball upon the green and again holed out with one putt. "I'm taking a five," I said, marking it on my card.

"I'm giving you a ten," he said, marking it on his card. "Five gesticulations on account of your pity."

QUESTION: Describe your reactions to this terrible injustice, Professor. Was there a red mist before your eyes? Did you turn giddy and wake up to find him lying lifeless at your feet? Just what happened?

ANSWER: Nothing, sir.

(*Sensation in the grand jury room.*)

QUESTION: Think again, Professor. Nothing?

ANSWER: I merely reflected that, in spite of his standing scientifically, Dr James T. Green was a moron and utterly devoid of morality and that I should take this into account. I did not lose my temper.

QUESTION: Did you snatch the card from his hands?

ANSWER: I took it, sir. I did not snatch it.

QUESTION: And then did you cram it down his throat?

ANSWER: I suggested that he eat it, sir, as it contained a falsehood in black and white, and Dr Green complied with my request.

QUESTION: Did you lay hands upon him, Professor? Remember, now, we are still talking about the third hole.

ANSWER: I think I did steady him a little by holding him about the neck and throat while he masticated and swallowed the card.

QUESTION: And then what?

ANSWER: Well, gentlemen, after that there is very little more to tell until we reached the sixteenth hole. Dr Green for some time made no further attempt to treat me unjustly and played in silence, acquiescing in the scores I had marked on my card. We were even as to holes, and it was a certainty that I was about to break a hundred. But I knew what was beneath this silence on Doc Green's part, and I did not trust it.

QUESTION: What do you mean? That you knew what he was thinking, although he did not speak?

ANSWER: Yes, sir. I knew just what kind of remarks he would have made if he had made any remarks.

QUESTION: Were these remarks which he suppressed derogatory remarks?

ANSWER: Yes, sir. Almost unbelievably so. They were deliberately intended to destroy my poise.

QUESTION: Did they do so, Professor?

ANSWER: I don't think so.

QUESTION: Go on, Professor.

ANSWER: At the sixteenth tee, as I drove off, this form of insult reached its climax. He accentuated his silence with a peculiar look, just as my club head was about to meet the ball. I knew what he meant. He knew that I knew it, and that I knew. I sliced into a bunker. He stood and watched me, as I stepped into the sand with my niblick—watched me with that look upon his face. I made three strokes at the ball and, as will sometimes happen even to the best of players, did not move it a foot. The fourth stroke drove it out of sight into the sand. The sixth stroke brought it to light again. Gentlemen, I did not lose my temper. I never do. But I admit that I did increase my tempo. I struck rapidly three more times at the ball. And all the time Doc Green was regarding me with that look, to which he now added a smile. Still I kept my temper, and he might be alive today if he had not spoken.

QUESTION (*by the foreman of the jury*): What did the man say at this trying time?

ANSWER: I know that you will not believe it is within the human heart to make the black remark that he made. And I hesitate to repeat it. But I have sworn to tell everything. What he said was, "Well, Professor, the club puts these bunkers here, and I suppose they have got to be used."

QUESTION (*by the foreman of the jury*): Was there something especially trying in the way he said it?

ANSWER: There was. He said it with an affectation of joviality.

QUESTION: You mean as if he thought he were making a joke, Professor?

ANSWER: Yes, sir.

QUESTION: What were your emotions at this point?

ANSWER: Well, sir, it came to me suddenly that I owed a duty to society; and for the sake of civilization I struck him with the niblick. It was an effort to reform him, gentlemen.

QUESTION: Why did you cover him with sand afterwards?

ANSWER: Well, I knew that if the crowd around the locker room discovered that I had hit him, they would insist on counting it as another stroke. And that is exactly what happened when the body was discovered— once again I was prevented from breaking a hundred.

THE DISTRICT ATTORNEY: Gentlemen of the jury, you have heard Professor Waddems' frank and open testimony in the case of Dr James T. Green. My own recommendation is that he be not only released, but complimented, as far as this count is returned. If ever a homicide was justifiable, this one was. And I suggest that you report no indictment against the Professor, without leaving your seats. Many of you will wish to get in at least nine holes before dinner. Tomorrow Professor Waddems will tell us what he knows about the case of Silas W. Amherst, the banker.

The district attorney has given me the following certified copy of my sworn testimony, and I am telling the story of this golf game to the public just as I told it in the grand jury room.

The Case of Silas W. Amherst, Banker

QUESTION: Professor Waddems, will you tell the jury just when it was that you first noted evidences of the criminal tendencies, amounting to total depravity, in the late Silas W. Amherst?

ANSWER: It was on the 30th of September, 1936, at 4:17 p.m.

QUESTION: Where were you when you first began to suspect that the man had such an evil nature?

ANSWER: On the Rivercliff golf course, sir, at the second hole.

QUESTION: A par-four hole, Professor?

ANSWER: It is called that, yes, sir; but it is unfairly trapped.

QUESTION: What is your usual score on this hole, Professor Waddems? Remember, you are on oath, and you have waived immunity in this inquiry.

ANSWER: I have never yet received fair treatment with regard to this hole. My normal score on this hole is five, with an occasional par four and sometimes a birdie three. But disgraceful tactics have always been employed against me on this hole to prevent me from playing my normal game.

QUESTION: Is it a water hole?

ANSWER: Yes, sir.

QUESTION: Is it the same water hole from which the

body of Silas W. Amherst was removed on October 3, 1936, a few days after he was last seen alone with you?

ANSWER: No, sir. That was the fifteenth hole. The water at the fifteenth hole is much deeper than the water at the second hole or the seventh hole. In the water at the fifteenth hole there are now several other bod——

QUESTION: Be careful, Professor! This inquiry is devoted entirely to Silas W. Amherst, and you are not compelled to incriminate or degrade yourself. Professor, are you a nervous, irritable, testy, violent person?

ANSWER: No, sir! No, sir! No, sir! And the man that dares to call me that is . . . (*A portion of Prof. Waddems' reply is stricken from the record.*)

QUESTION: Quietly, Professor, quietly! Tell these gentlemen how you gained the unruffled patience and philosophic calm that have made you the great golfer that you are.

ANSWER: For twenty-five years I lectured on philosophy and psychology at various universities. And I apply these principles to my golf game.

QUESTION: In spite of your thorough scientific knowledge of the game, have you ever broken a hundred?

ANSWER: Yes, sir, many times.

QUESTION: Think, Professor!

ANSWER: Yes, sir; yes, sir; yes, sir!

QUESTION: Mildly, please, Professor! Quietly! I will put the question in a different way. Professor, has any opponent with whom you played ever *admitted* that you broke a hundred, or has any card that you turned in after playing around alone been credited, if it showed you *had* broken a hundred?

ANSWER: I don't remember, sir. My game has been misrepresented and persecuted for years at Rivercliff.

QUESTION: To return to Mr Amherst. Tell the jury exactly what happened at the second hole which revealed the man's irreclaimable blackness of character.

ANSWER: Well, sir, I teed up for my drive and addressed the ball. And just as I brought my club back, and it was poised for the down stroke, he said to me:

"Professor, you're driving with a brassie, aren't you?"

I gave him a look of mild expostulation, checked the drive, and stood in front of the ball again.

"I don't think your stance is right, Professor," he said. "Let me show you the proper stance—you don't mind my showing you, do you, Professor?"

Then he proceeded to show me—and I may say in passing that his theories were entirely faulty.

"I noticed on the first tee," he went on, "that you didn't understand how to pivot. You want to get your body into it, Professor. Like this," and he made a swing in demonstration.

"Your instruction, Mr Amherst," I said politely, "is entirely gratuitous and all wrong."

"I thought you'd be glad to have me show you, Professor," he said. "And if I were you, I wouldn't play that new ball on this water hole. Here, I'll lend you a floater."

And the man actually took from his bag a floater,

removed my ball, and teed up the one he had lent me.

"Now, Professor," he said, "a little more freedom in your swing. Keep your eye on the ball and don't let your hands come through ahead of the club. I noticed you had a tendency that way. I think your grip is wrong, Professor. Oh yes, certainly wrong! Here, let me show you the correct grip. And keep your head down, keep your head down!"

QUESTION: Was it then, Professor, that the tragedy occurred?

ANSWER: No, sir! No, sir! No, sir!

QUESTION: Quietly, Professor, quietly! You remained calm?

ANSWER: I am always calm! I never lose my temper! I am always patient! Self-contained! Restrained! Philosophical! Unperturbed! Nothing excites me! Nothing, I say, nothing! Nothing! Nothing! Nothing!

QUESTION: There, there, Professor, easily, easily now! What happened next?

ANSWER: I took a driving iron from my bag and addressed the ball again. I——

QUESTION: Just a moment, Professor. Why did you not continue with the brassie?

ANSWER: It was broken, sir.

QUESTION: Broken? How? I do not understand. How did it become broken?

ANSWER: I do not remember.

QUESTION: Between Mr Amherst's instruction with the brassie and your taking the driving iron from the bag, as I understand it, the brassie was somehow broken. Please fill up this interval for the jury. What happened?

ANSWER: I can't recall, sir.

QUESTION: Come, come, Professor! How was the brassie broken?

ANSWER: It hit the sandbox, sir.

QUESTION: How could it hit the sandbox?

ANSWER: Well, it was an old brassie, and after I had made a few practice swings with it, I decided that it was poorly balanced and that I had better get rid of it once and for all. I did not wish to give it to a caddie, for I do not think it is fair to give poor clubs to these boys who are earnestly striving to educate themselves to be professionals; they are poor boys, for the most part, and we who are in better circumstances should see that they have a fair start in life. So I broke the brassie against the sandbox and took my driving iron, and——

QUESTION: Just a minute, Professor! These practice strokes that you made with the brassie, were there five or six of them?

ANSWER: I don't recollect, sir.

QUESTION: Did any one of them hit the ball?

ANSWER: No, sir! No, sir! No, sir! The brassie never touched the ball! The ball moved because there was a bent twig under it—this man Amherst had teed up his floater for me with a pat of sand upon a bent twig— and the twig straightened up and moved the sand, and the ball rolled off of it.

QUESTION (*by the foreman of the jury*): Professor

Waddems, how far did the ball roll when the twig straightened up?

ANSWER: Well, sir, it had been teed up at the very edge of the driving green, and the ground is pretty high there, and the ball rolled down the slope, and it gained a great deal of momentum as it rolled down the slope, like an avalanche as it comes rolling down a mountain-side, and at the bottom of the slope it struck a rut in the road the work-and-upkeep wagons use on the course, and that rut connects with the asphalt drive that leads in to the clubhouse, and when the ball struck the asphalt road it had already gained so much momentum that it rolled for some distance along the asphalt road, and then it crashed into the underbrush near the road and hit a sapling and bounded over onto the first fairway, all on account of the slope of the ground, for it had never been touched with the brassie at all.

QUESTION: Professor, did this happen to the ball five or six times before you discarded the brassie and took the driving iron?

ANSWER: No, sir. I only recall three times.

QUESTION: Go on, Professor. After these practice strokes, and your breaking of the brassie, you took the driving iron. What happened then?

ANSWER: Then Mr Amherst stepped up and said to me, "Professor, let me give you a few tips about iron play. And you must keep your head down, keep your head down!"

QUESTION: Did you lose your temper then?

Answer: I never lose my temper! Never! Never! Never!

Question: Quietly, now, Professor, quietly! Go on.

Answer: I made a magnificent drive, which cleared the water jump, and my second shot was on the green. I holed out with two putts. "A par four," I said, marking it on my card.

"You mean nine," said this man Amherst. Gentlemen, he had the effrontery to claim that the five practice swings I had made with the brassie, just simply to humor him in his demonstrations, were actual golf strokes!

(*Sensation in the grand jury room. Cries of "Outrageous!" "Impossible!" "The Dastard!" from various grand jurymen. The outburst quelled with difficulty by the district attorney.*)

Question (*by the foreman of the jury*): Professor Waddems, did you end it all then?

Answer: No, sir. I kept my self-control. Gentlemen, I am always for peace! I am a meek person. I am mild. I will endure persecution to a point beyond anything that is possible to a man who has not had my years of training in philosophy and applied psychology. I merely got another caddie and proceeded with the game, yielding the point to Mr Amherst for the sake of peace.

Question: Got another caddie?

Answer: Yes, sir. The one I started out with was injured.

Question: How, Professor?

Answer: I don't remember.

QUESTION: Think, Professor! Was it by a fall?

ANSWER: Oh yes, now I recollect! It *was* by a fall. The caddie fell from a tree just beyond the second green and broke his shoulder.

QUESTION: What was he doing in the tree?

ANSWER: He had retired to the top of the tree under a peculiar misapprehension, sir. He had agreed with Mr Amherst with regard to the question as to whether I should take nine strokes or a par four; and I think he misinterpreted some sudden motion of mine as a threat.

QUESTION: A motion with a golf club?

ANSWER: It may have been, sir. I had a club in my hand, and I remember that my mind at the moment was engrossed with a problem connected with the underlying psychology of the full swing with wooden clubs.

QUESTION: Well, Professor, the caddie is now at the top of the tree, laboring under a misapprehension. What caused his fall?

ANSWER: I think the wooden club must have slipped somehow from my hands, sir. It flew to the top of the tree and disturbed his balance, causing him to fall.

QUESTION: Was he a good caddie?

ANSWER: There are no good caddies, sir.

(*Ripple of acquiescent laughter goes round the grand jury room.*)

QUESTION: Then, Professor, you went on to the next driving green. Tell what happened from this point on to the fifteenth hole, where the body of Silas W. Amherst was found four days later.

ANSWER: Advice, sir, advice! That's what happened! Advice! One long, intolerable gehenna of gratuitous advice! Gentlemen, I don't know whether any of you ever had the misfortune to play golf with the late Silas W. Amherst, but if you had——

(*Cries from various grand jurors: "Yes, yes, I played with him!" "Ataboy, Professor!" "I knew him, Prof!" etc., etc. District attorney begs for order; witness continues.*)

ANSWER: Advice! Advice! Advice! And always the fiendish malignity of the man concealed under a cloak of helpful friendliness! Advice! Advice! Advice! And to me! I, who have studied the basic principles of the game more thoroughly than any other man in America today! Gentlemen, if I were not the most patient man in the world, Silas W. Amherst would have bit the dust twenty times between the second and the fifteenth holes that day! His explanations—to me! His continual babble and chatter! His demonstrations! Every club I took from my bag, he *explained* to me! Gentlemen, some of them were clubs that I had designed myself and had had manufactured to fit my own original theories with regard to golf! But I kept my temper! I never lose my temper! Never! Never! Never!

QUESTION: Does any particularly insulting phrase of advice stand out in your memory, Professor?

ANSWER: Yes, sir! A dozen times on every hole he would cry to me as I addressed the ball, "Keep your head down, Professor, keep your head down!"

THE DISTRICT ATTORNEY: Please sit down, Professor; and do not bang on the chairs with your walking stick as you talk. We cannot hear your testimony.

THE PROFESSOR: Yes, sir. Well, at the fifteenth hole, while he was standing on the edge of the water, looking for a ball——

QUESTION: Professor, is it true that the fifteenth hole at Rivercliff is really a pool, fed by subterranean springs, and so deep that no plummet has ever sounded its bottom?

ANSWER: Exactly, sir. As Silas W. Amherst stood on the edge of it, it occurred to me that perhaps the man's conscience had awakened and that he was going to commit suicide for the good of the human race, gentlemen. And so I gave him a little pat of approval—on the back; and he fell in. Gentlemen, he judged himself and executed himself, and I still approve.

QUESTION: Would you mind telling the jurors, Professor, just what Mr Amherst said immediately before you patted him approvingly on the back?

ANSWER: He said, "You just stick to me, Professor, and do as I show you, and I'll make some kind of golfer out of you yet."

QUESTION: Did he try to struggle to land, and did you hold his head under water?

ANSWER: Yes, sir, I generously assisted him in his purpose to that extent.

QUESTION: What did you say while you were assisting him?

ANSWER: I said, "Keep your head down, Mr Amherst, keep your head down!"

THE FOREMAN OF THE JURY: Mr District Attorney, speaking for the other members of this jury as well as for myself, it is ridiculous to consider the matter of finding any true bill or indictment of any sort against Professor Waddems in the case of the late Mr Amherst. The pat of approval was more than justified, and we consider Professor Waddems a public benefactor.

THE DISTRICT ATTORNEY: Tomorrow we will take up the case of Willie, alias "Freckled," Briggs, the caddie who met his death on October 4, 1936, at the Rivercliff Country Club. I suggest that the slight rain we have had today, which is happily over with, should contribute greatly to what is known as a good brassie lie on the fairways. You are dismissed for the day.

THE SADDEST MAN

THE bench, the barrel, and the cracker box in front of Hennery McNabb's general store held three men, all of whom seemed to be thinking. Two of them were not only thinking but chewing tobacco as well. The third, more enterprising than the other two, more active, was exerting himself prodigiously. He was thinking, chewing tobacco, and whittling all at the same time.

Two of the men were native and indigenous to Hazelton. They drew their sustenance from the black soil of the Illinois prairie on which the little village was perched. They were as calm and placid as the growing corn in the fields round about, as solid and self-possessed and leisurely as the bullheads in the little creek down at the end of Main Street.

The third man was a stranger, somewhere between six and eight feet high and so slender that one might have expected the bones to pop through the skin, if one's attention had not been arrested by the skin itself. For he was covered and contained by a most peculiar skin. It was dark and rubbery-looking rather than leathery, and it seemed to be endowed with a life of its own almost independent of the rest of the man's anatomy. When a fly perched upon his cheek he did not raise his hand to brush it off. The man himself did not move at all. But his skin moved. His skin rose up, wrinkled, twitched, rippled beneath the fly's feet, and the fly took alarm and went away from there as if an earthquake had broken loose under it. He was a sad-looking man. He looked sadder than the mummy of an Egyptian king who died brooding on what a long dry spell lay ahead of him.

It was this third man of whom the other two men were thinking, this melancholy stranger who sat and stared through the thick, humid heat of the July day at nothing at all, with grievous eyes, his ego motion-less beneath the movements of his rambling skin. He had driven up the road thirty minutes before in a flivver, had bought some chewing tobacco of Hennery McNabb, and had set himself down in front of the store and chewed tobacco in silence ever since.

Finally Ben Grevis, the village gravedigger and janitor of the church, broke through the settled still-ness with a question:

"Mister," he said, "you ain't done nothing you're afraid of being arrested for, hev you?"

The stranger slowly turned his head toward Ben and made a negative sign. He did not shake his head in negation. He moved the skin of his forehead from left to right and back again three or four times. And his eyebrows moved as his skin moved. But his eyes re-mained fixed and melancholy.

"Sometimes," suggested Hennery McNabb, who had almost tired himself out whittling, "a man's sys-tem needs overhaulin', same as a horse's needs drench-in'. I don't aim to push my goods onto no man, but if you was feelin' anyway sick, inside or out, I got some of Splain's Liniment for Man and Beast in there that might fix you up."

"I ain't sick," said the stranger, in a low and gentle voice.

"I never seen many fellers that looked as sad as you do," volunteered Ben Grevis. "There was a mighty sad-lookin' tramp, that resembled you in the face some, was arrested here for bein' drunk eight or nine years ago, only he wasn't as tall as you an' his skin was different. After Si Emery, our city marshal, had kep' him in the lock-up over Sunday and turned him loose again, it come to light he was wanted over in I'way for killin' a feller with a piece of railroad iron."

"I ain't killed anybody with any railroad iron over in I'way," said the lengthy man. And he added, with a sigh, "Nor nowheres else, neither."

Hennery McNabb, who disagreed with everyone on principle—he was the village atheist, and proud of it—addressed himself to Ben Grevis. "This feller ain't nigh as sad-lookin' as that tramp looked," said Hennery. "I've knowed any number of fellers sadder-lookin' than this feller here."

"I didn't say this feller here was the saddest-lookin' feller I ever seen," said Ben Grevis. "All I meant was that he is sadder-lookin' than the common run of fellers." While Hennery disagreed with all the world, Ben seldom disagreed with anyone but Hennery. They would argue by the hour, on religious matters, always beginning with Hennery's challenge: "Ben Grevis, tell me just one thing if you can, *where* did Cain get his wife?" and always ending with Ben's statement: "I believe the Book from kiver to kiver."

The tall man with the educated skin—it was educated, very evidently, for with a contraction of the hide on the back of his hand he nonchalantly picked up a shaving that had blown his way—spoke to Ben and Hennery in the soft and mild accents that seemed habitual to him:

"Where did you two see sadder-lookin' fellers than I be?"

"Over in Indianny," said Hennery, "there's a man so sad that you're one of these here laughin' jackasses 'longside o' him."

And, being encouraged, Hennery proceeded.

This here feller (said Hennery McNabb) lived over in Brown County, Indianny, but he didn't come from there original. He come from down in Kentucky somewheres and his name was Peevy, Bud Peevy. He was one of them long, lank fellers, like you, stranger, but he wasn't as long, and his skin didn't sort o' wander around and wag itself like it was a tail.

It was from the mountain districts he come. I was visitin' a brother of mine in the county-seat town of Brown County then, and this Bud Peevy was all swelled up with pride when I first knowed him. He was proud of two things. One was that he was the champeen cornlicker drinker in Kentucky. It was so he give himself out. And the other thing he was prouder yet of. It was the fact, if fact it was, that he was the Decidin' Vote in a national election—that there election you all remember, the first time Bryan run for President and McKinley was elected.

This here Bud Peevy, you understand, wasn't really sad when I first knowed him: he only *looked* sad. His sadness that matched his innard feelin's up to his outward looks come onto him later. He was all-fired proud when I first knowed him. He went expandin' and extendin' of himself around everywheres tellin' them Indianny people how it was him, personal, that elected McKinley and saved the country from that there free-silver ruination. And the fuller he was of licker, the longer he made this here story, and the fuller, as you might say, of increditable, strange events.

Accordin' to him, on that election day in 1896 he hadn't planned to go and vote, for it was quite a ways to the polls from his place and his horse had fell lame and he didn't feel like walkin'. He figgered his district would go safe for McKinley, anyhow, and he wouldn't need to vote. He was a strong Republican, and when a Kentuckian is a Republican there ain't no stronger kind.

But along about four o'clock in the afternoon a man comes ridin' up to his house with his horse all a lather of foam and sweat, and the horse was one of these here Kentucky thoroughbred race horses that musta traveled nigh a mile a minute, to hear Bud Peevy tell of it, and that horse gives one groan like a human bein' and falls dead at Bud Peevy's feet afore the rider can say a word, and the rider is stunned.

But Bud Peevy knowed him for a Republican county committeeman, and he poured some corn licker down his throat and he revived to life again. The feller yells to Bud as soon as he can get his breath to go to town and vote, quick, as the polls will close in an hour, and everybody else in that district has voted but Bud, and everyone has been kep' track of, and the vote is a tie.

It's twelve miles to the pollin' place from Bud's farm in the hills, and it is a rough country, but Bud strikes out runnin' acrost hills and valleys with three pints of corn licker in his pockets for to refresh himself from time to time. Bud, he allowed he was the best runner in Kentucky, and he wouldn'ta had any trouble, even if he did have to run acrost mountains and hurdle rocks, to make the twelve miles in an hour, but there was a lot of cricks and rivers in that country and there had been a gosh-a'mighty big rain the night before and all them cricks had turned into rivers and all them rivers had turned into roarin' oceans and Niagara cata-rac's. But Bud, he allows he is the best swimmer in Kentucky, and when he comes to a stream he takes a swig of corn licker and jumps in and swims acrost, boots and all—for he was runnin' in his big cowhides, strikin' sparks of fire from the mountains with every leap he made.

Five times he was shot at by Democrats in the first six miles, and in the seventh mile the shootin' was almost continual, and three or four times he was hit, but he kep' on. It seems the Democrats had got wind he had been sent for to turn the tide, and a passel of 'em was out among the hills with rifles to stop him if they could. But he is in too much of a hurry to bandy words with 'em, and he didn't have his gun along, which he regretted, he says, as he is the best gun fighter in Kentucky and he keeps on a-runnin' and a-swimmin' and a-jumpin' cricks and a-hurdlin' rocks with the bullets whizzin' around him and the lightnin' strikin' in his path, for another big storm had come up, and no power on this here earth could head him off, he says, for it come to him like a Voice from on High he was the preordained messenger and hero who was goin' to turn the tide and save the country from this here free-silver ruination. About two miles from the pollin' place, jist as he jumps into the last big river, two men plunges into the water after him with dirks, and one of them he gets quick, but the other one drags Bud under the water, stabbin' and jabbin' at him. There is a terrible stabbin' and stickin' battle 'way down under the water, which is runnin' so fast that big stones the size of a cow is being rolled downstream, but Bud he don't mind the stones, and he can swim under water as well as on top of it, he says, and he's the best knife fighter in Kentucky, he says, and he soon fixes that feller and swims to shore with his knife in his teeth, and now he's only got one more mountain to cross.

But a kind of hurricane has sprung up and turned into a cyclone in there among the hills, and as he goes over the top of that last mountain, lickety-split, in the dark and wind and rain, he blunders into a whole pas-sel of rattlesnakes that has got excited by the elements. But he fit his way through 'em, thankin' God he had nearly a quart of licker left to take for the eight or ten bites he got, and next there rose up in front of him two of them big brown bears, and they was wild with rage because the storm had been slingin' boulders at 'em. One of them bears he sticked with his knife and made short work of, but the other one give him quite a tussel, Bud says, afore he conquered it and straddled it. And it was a lucky thing for him, he says, that he caught that bear in time, he was gittin' a leetle weak with loss of blood and snakebites and battlin' with the elements. Bud, he is the best rider in Kentucky, and it wasn't thirty seconds afore that bear knowed a master was a-ridin' of it, and in five minutes more Bud, he gal-lops up to that pollin' place, right through the heart of the hurricane, whippin' that bear with rattlesnakes to make it go faster, and he jumps off and cracks his boot heels together and gives a yell and casts the de-cidin' vote into the ballot box. He had made it with nearly ten seconds to spare.

Well, accordin' to Bud Peevy that there one vote carries the day for McKinley in that county, and not only in that county alone, but in that electorial district, and that electorial district gives McKinley the state of Kentucky, which no Republican had ever carried Ken-tucky for President for afore. And two or three other states was hangin' back keepin' their polls open late to see how Kentucky would go, and when it was flashed by telegraph all over the country that Bud Peevy was carryin' Kentucky for McKinley, them other states joined in with Kentucky and cast their electorial votes that-a-way, too, and McKinley was elected President.

So Bud figgers he has jist naturally elected that man President and saved the country—he is the one that was the Decidin' Vote for this whole derned republic. And, as I said, he loves to tell about it. It was in 1896 that Bud saved the country, and it was in 1900 that he moved to Brown County, Indianny, and started in with his oratin' about what a great man he was, and givin' his political opinions about this, that and the other thing, like he mighta been President himself. Bein' a Decidin' Vote that-a-way made him think he jist about run this country with his ideas.

He's been hangin' around the streets in his new home, the county town of Brown County, for five or six weeks, in the summer of 1900, tellin' what a great feller he is, and bein' admired by everybody, when one day the news comes that the U. S. census for 1900 has been pretty nigh finished, and that the Center of Population for the whole country falls in Brown County. Well, you can understand that's calculated to make folks in that county pretty darned proud.

But the proudest of them all was a feller by the name of Ezekiel Humphreys. It seems these here government sharks had it figgered out that the center of population fell right onto where this here Zeke Humphreys' farm was, four or five miles out of town.

And Zeke, he figgers that he, himself, personal, has become the Center of Population.

Zeke hadn't never been an ambitious man. He hadn't never gone out and courted any glory like that, nor schemed for it nor thought of it. But he was a feller that thought well enough of himself, too. He had been a steady, hard-workin' kind of man all his life, mindin' his own business and payin' his debts, and when this here glory comes to him, bein' chose out of ninety millions of people, as you might say, to be the one and only Center of Population, he took it as his just due and was proud of it.

"You see how the office seeks the man, if the man is worthy of it!" says Zeke. And everybody liked Zeke that knowed him, and was glad of his glory.

Well, one day this here Decidin' Vote, Bud Peevy, comes to town to fill himself up on licker and tell how he saved the country, and he is surprised because he don't get nobody to listen to him. And pretty soon he sees the reason for it. There's a crowd of people on Main Street all gathered around Zeke Humphreys and all congratulatin' him on being the Center of Population. And they was askin' his opinion on politics and things. Zeke is takin' it modest and sensible, but like a man that knowed he deserved it, too. Bud Peevy, he listens for a while, and he sniffs and snorts, but nobody pays any 'tention to him. Finally, he can't keep his mouth shut any longer, and he says:

"Politics! Politics! To hear you talk, a fellow'd think you really got a claim to talk about politics!"

Zeke, he never was any trouble hunter, but he never run away from it, neither.

"Mebby," says Zeke, not het up any, but right serious and determined-like, "mebby you got more claim to talk about politics than I have?"

"I shore have," says Bud Peevy. "I reckon I got more claim to be hearkened to about politics than any other man in this here whole country. I'm the Decidin' Vote of this here country, I am!"

"Well, gosh-ding my melts!" says Zeke Humphreys. "You ain't proud of yourself, nor nothin', are you?"

"No prouder nor what I got a right to be," says Bud Peevy, "considerin' what I done."

"Oh yes, you be!" says Zeke Humphreys. "You been proudin' yourself around here for weeks now all on account o' that decidin'-vote business. And *anybody* mighta been a Decidin' Vote. A Decidin' Vote don't amount to nothin' 'longside a Center of Population."

"Where would your derned population be if I hadn't went and saved this here country for 'em?" asks Bud Peevy.

"Be?" says Zeke. "They'd be right where they be now, if you'd never been born nor heard tell on, that's where they'd be. And I'd be the center of 'em, jist like I be now!"

"And what *air* you now?" says Bud Peevy, mighty mean and insultin'-like. "You ain't nothin' but a accident, you ain't! What I got, I fit for and I earnt. But you ain't nothin' but a happenin'!"

Them seemed like mighty harsh words to Zeke, for

he figgered his glory was due to him on account of the uprighteous life he always led, and so he says:

"Mister, anybody that says I ain't nothin' but a happenin' is a liar."

"I kin lick my weight in rattlesnakes," yells Bud Peevy, "and I've done it afore this! And I tells you once again, and flings it in your face, that you ain't nothin' but a accidental happenin'!"

"You're a liar, then!" says Zeke.

With that Bud Peevy jerks his coat off and spits onto his hands.

"Set yo'self, man," says he; "the whirlwind's comin'!" And he makes a rush at Zeke. Bud is a good deal taller'n Zeke, but Zeke is sort o' bricky-red and chunky like a Dutch Reformed Church, and when this here Peevy comes onto him with a jump Zeke busts him one right onto the eye. It makes an uncheerful noise like I heard one time when Dan Lively, the butcher acrost the street there, hit a steer in the head with a sledge hammer. Bud, he sets down sudden and looks surprised out of the eye that hadn't went to war yet. But he musta figgered it was a accident, for he don't set there long. He jumps up and rushes again.

"I'm a wildcat! I'm a wildcat!"

And Zeke, he collisions his fist with the other eye, and Bud sets down the second time. I won't say this here Zeke's hands was as big as a quarter of beef. The fact is, they wasn't that big. But I seen that fight myself, and there was somethin' about the size and shape of his fist when it was doubled up that kind o' *reminded* me of a quarter of beef. Only his fists was harder than a quarter of beef. I guess Zeke's fists was about as hard as a hickory log that has been gettin' itself soaked and dried and seasoned for two or three years. I heard a story about Zeke and a mule that kicked him one time, but I didn't see it myself and I dunno as it's all true. The word was that Zeke jist picked up that mule after it kicked him and frowned at it and told it if it ever done that again he would jist naturally pull off the leg that it kicked him with and turn it loose to hop away on three legs, and he cuffed that mule thorough and thoughtful and then he took it by one hind leg and fore leg and jounced it against a stone barn and told it to behave its fool self. It always seemed to me that story had been stretched a mite, but that was one of the stories they telled on Zeke.

But this here Bud Peevy is game. He jumps up again with his two eyes lookin' like a skillet full of tripe and onions and makes another rush at Zeke. And this time he gets his hands onto Zeke, and they rastles back and forth. But Bud, while he is a strong fellow, he ain't no ways as strong as a mule, even if he is jist as sudden and wicked, so Zeke throws him down two or three times. Bud, he kicks Zeke right vicious and spiteful into the stomach, and when he done that Zeke began to get a little cross. So he throwed Bud down again, and this time he set on top of him.

"Now, then," says Zeke, bangin' Bud's head onto the sidewalk, "am I a happenin', or am I on purpose?"

"Lemme up," says Bud. "Leggo my whiskers and

lemme up! You ain't licked me any, but them ol' wounds I got savin' this country is goin' to bust open ag'in. I kin feel 'em bustin'."

"I didn't start this," says Zeke, "but I'm a-goin' to finish it. Now, then, am I a accident, or was I meant?"

"It's a accident you ever got me down," says Bud, "whether you are a accident yourself or not."

Zeke jounces his head on the sidewalk some more, and he says, "You answer better nor that! You go further! You tell me whether I'm on purpose or not!"

"You was meant for somethin'," says Bud, "but you can't make me say what! You can bang my head off and I won't say what. Two or three of them bullets went into my neck right where you're bendin' it, and I feel them ol' wounds bustin' open."

"I don't believe you got no ol' wounds," says Zeke, "and I don't believe you ever saved no country, and I'm gonna keep you here till I've banged some sense and politeness into your head."

Bud, he gives a yell and a twist and bites Zeke's wrist; Zeke slapped him some, and Bud ketched one of Zeke's fingers into his mouth and nigh bit it off afore Zeke got it loose. Zeke, he was a patient man and right thoughtful and judicious, but he had got kind o' cross when Bud kicked him into the stomach, and now this biting made him a leetle mite crosser. I cal'ated if Bud wasn't careful he'd get Zeke really riled up pretty soon and get his fool self hurt. Zeke, he takes Bud by the ears and slams his head till I thought the boards in the sidewalk was goin' to be busted.

"Now, then," says Zeke, lettin' up for a minute, "has the Center of Population got a right to talk politics, or ain't he? You say he is got a right, or I mebby will fergit myself and get kind o' rough with you."

"This here country I saved is a free country," says Bud Peevy, kind o' sick and feeble, "and anyone that lives in this here country I saved has got a right to talk politics, I reckon."

Zeke, he took that for an answer and got good-natured and let Bud up. Bud, he wipes the blood off'n his face and ketches his breath an' gits mean again right away.

"If my constitution hadn't been undermined savin' this here country," says Bud, "you never coulda got me down like that! And you ain't heard the end of this argyment yet, neither! I'm a-goin' for my gun, and we'll shoot it out!"

But the townspeople interfered and give Bud to understand he couldn't bring no guns into a fight, like mebby he woulda done in them mountain regions he was always talkin' about; an' told him if he was to start gunnin' around they would get up a tar-and-feather party and he would be the reception committee. They was all on Zeke's side, and they'd all got kind o' tired listenin' to Bud Peevy, anyhow. Zeke was their own home-town man, and so they backed him. All that glory had come to Brown County, and they wasn't goin' to see it belittled by no feller from another place.

Bud Peevy, for two or three weeks, can't understand his glory has left him, and he goes braggin' around worse than ever. But people only grins and turns away; nobody will hark to him when he talks. When Bud tries to tell his story it gets to be quite the thing to look at him and say, "Lemme up! Leggo my whiskers! Lemme up!"—like he said when Zeke Humphreys had him down. And so it was he come to be a byword around town. Kids would yell at him on the street to plague him, and he would get mad and chase them kids, and when folks would see him runnin' after the kids they would yell, "Hey! Hey, Bud Peevy! You could go faster if you was to ride a bear!" Or else they would yell, "Whip yourself with a rattlesnake, Bud, and get up some speed!"

His glory had been so big and so widespread for so long that when it finally went there jist wasn't a darned thing left to him. His heart busted in his bosom. He wouldn't talk about nothin'. He jist slinked around. He was most pitiful because he wasn't used to misfortune like some people.

And he couldn't pack up his goods and move away from that place. For he had come there to live with a married daughter and his son-in-law, and if he left there he would have to get a steady job working at somethin' and support himself. And Bud didn't want to risk that. For that wild run he made the time he saved the country left him strained clean down to the innards of his constitution, he says, and he wa'n't fit to work. But the thing that put the finishing touches onto him was when a single daughter that he had fell in love with Zeke Humphreys, who was a widower, and married herself to him. His own flesh and blood has disowned him, Bud says. So he turns sad, and he was the saddest man I ever seen. He was sadder than you look to be, stranger.

The stranger with the educated skin breathed a gentle sigh at the conclusion of Hennery's tale of the Deciding Vote and the Center of Population, and then he said:

"I don't doubt Bud Peevy was a sad man. But there's sadder things than what happened to Bud Peevy. There's things that touches the heart closer."

"Stranger," said Ben Grevis, "you've said it! But Hennery, here, don't know anything about the heart bein' touched."

Hennery McNabb seemed to enjoy the implication, rather than to resent it. Ben Grevis continued:

"A sadder thing than what happened to Bud Peevy is goin' on a good deal nearer home than Indianny.

"I ain't the kind of a feller that goes running to Indianny and to Kentucky and all over the known earth for examples of sadness, nor nothin' else. We got as good a country right here in Illinois as there is on top of the earth, and I'm one that always sticks up for home folks and home industries. Hennery, here, ain't got any patriotism. And he ain't got any judgment. He don't know what's in front of him. But right here in our home county, not five miles from where we are, sets a case of sadness that is one of the saddest I ever seen or knowed about.

"Hennery, here, he don't know how sad it is, for he's got no finer feelin's. A freethinker like Hennery can't be expected to have no finer feelin's. And this case is a case of a woman."

"A woman!" sighed the stranger. "If a woman is mixed up with it, it could have finer feelin's and sadness in it!" And a ripple of melancholy ran over him from head to foot.

This here woman (said Ben Grevis) lives over to Hickory Grove, in the woods, and everybody for miles around calls her Widder Watson.

Widder Watson, she has buried four or five husbands, and you can see her any day that it ain't rainin' settin' in the door of her little house, smokin' of her corncob pipe and lookin' at their graves and speculatin' and wonderin'. I talked with her a good deal from time to time durin' the last three or four years, and the things she is speculatin' on is life and death, and them husbands she has buried, and children. But that ain't what makes her so sad. It's wishin' for somethin' that, it seems like, never can be, that is makin' her so sad.

She has got eighteen or twenty children, Widder Watson has, runnin' around them woods. Them woods is jist plumb full of her children. You wouldn't dare for to try to shoot a rabbit anywhere near them woods for fear of hittin' one.

And all them children has got the most beautiful and peculiar names, that Widder Watson got out of these here drugstore almanacs. She's been a great reader all her life, Widder Watson has, but all her readin' has been done in these here almanacs. You know how many different kinds of almanacs there always are layin' around drugstores, I guess. Well, every two or three months Widder Watson goes to town and gets a new bale of them almanacs, and then she sets and reads 'em. She goes to drugstores in towns as far as twelve or fifteen miles away to keep herself supplied.

She never cared much for readin' novels and story papers, she tells me. What she wants is somethin' that has got some true information in it, about the way the sun rises, and the tides in the oceans she has never saw, and when the eclipses is going to be, and different kinds of diseases new and old, and receipts for preserves and true stories about how this or that wonderful remedy come to be discovered. Mebby it was discovered by the Injuns in this country, or mebby it was discovered by them there Egyptians in the old country away back in King Pharaoh's time, and mebby she's got some of the same sort of yarbs and plants right there in her own woods. Well, Widder Watson, she likes that kind of readin', and she knows all about the Seven Wonders of the World, and all the organs and ornaments inside the human carcass, and the kind o' pains they are likely to have, and all about what will happen to you if the stars says this or that, and how long the Mississippi River is, and a lot of them old-time prophecies of signs and marvels what is to come to pass yet. You know about what the readin' is in them almanacs, mebby.

Widder Watson, she has got a natural likin' for fine

words, jist the same as some has got a gift for hand paintin' or playin' music or recitin' pieces of poetry or anything like that. And so it was quite natural, when her kids come along, she names 'em after the names in her favorite readin' matter. And she gets so she thinks more of the names of them kids than of nearly anything else. I ain't sayin' she thinks more of the names than she does of the kids, but she likes the names right next to the kids. Every time she had a baby she used to sit and think for weeks and weeks, so she tells me, for to get a good name for that baby, and select and select and select out of them almanacs.

Her oldest girl, that everybody calls Zody, is named Zodiac by rights. And then there's Carty, whose real name is Cartilege, and Anthy, whose full name is Anthrax, and so on. There's Peruna and Epidermis and Epidemic and Pisces.

I dunno as I can remember all them swell names. There's Perry, whose real name is Perihelion, and there's Whitsuntide and Tonsillitis and Opodeldoc and a lot more—I never could remember all them kids.

And there ain't goin' to be no more on 'em, for the fact of the matter seems to be that Widder Watson ain't likely to ever get another husband. It's been about four years since Jim Watson, her last one, died and was buried in there amongst the hickory second-growth and hazel bushes, and since that day there ain't been nobody come along that road a-courtin' Widder Watson. And that's what makes her sad. She can't understand it, never havin' been without a husband for so

long before, and she sets and grieves and grieves and
smokes her corncob pipe and speculates and grieves
some more.

Now don't you get no wrong idea about Widder
Watson. She ain't so all-fired crazy about men. It ain't
that. That ain't what makes her grieve. She is sad because she wants another baby to pin a name to.

For she has got the most lovely name out of a new
almanac for that there kid that will likely never be
born, and she sets there day after day, and far into the
night, lookin' at them graves in the brush, and talkin'
to the clouds and stars, and sayin' that name over and
over to herself, and sighin' and weepin' because that
lovely name will be lost and unknown and wasted for-
evermore, with no kid to tack it onto.

And she hopes and yearns and grieves for another
man to marry her and wonders why none of 'em never
does. Well, I can see why they don't. The truth is, Widder Watson don't fix herself up much any more. She
goes barefooted most of the time in warm weather, and
since she got so sadlike she don't comb her hair much.
And them corncob pipes of hern ain't none too savory.
But I s'pose she thinks of herself as bein' jist the same
way she was the last time she took the trouble to look
into the lookin' glass, and she can't understand it.

"Damn the men, Ben," she says to me, the last time
I was by there, "what's the matter with 'em all? Ain't
they got no sense any more? I never had no trouble
ketchin' a man before this! But here I been settin' for
three or four years, with eighty acres of good land

acrost the road there, and a whole passel o' young uns to work it, and no man comes to court me. There was a feller along here two-three months ago I did have some hopes on. He come a-palaverin' and a-blarneyin' along, and he stayed to dinner and I made him some apple dumplin's, and he et an' et and palavered.

"But it turned out he was really makin' up to that gal, Zody, of mine. It made me so darned mad, Ben, I runned him off the place with Jeff Parker's shotgun that is hangin' in there, and then I took a hickory sprout to that there Zody and tanned her good for en-couragin' of him. You remember Jeff Parker, Ben? He was my second. You wasn't thinkin' of gettin' married ag'in yourself, was you, Ben?"

I told her I wasn't. That there eighty acres is good land, and they ain't no mortgages on it, nor nothin', but the thought of bein' added to that collection in amongst the hazel brush and hickory sprouts is enough for to hold a man back. And the Widder Watson, she don't seem to realize she orter fix herself up a little mite. But I'm sorry for her, jist the same. There she sets and mourns, sayin' that name over and over to herself, and a-grievin' and a-hopin', and all the time she knows it ain't much use to hope. And a sadder sight than you will see over there to Hickory Grove ain't to be found in the whole of the state of Illinois.

"That is a mighty sad picture you have drawed," said the stranger, when Ben Grevis had finished, "but

I'm a sadder man for a man than that there woman
is for a woman."

He wrinkled all over, he almost grinned, if one could
think of him as grinning, when he mentioned "that
there woman." It was as if he tasted some ulterior jest,
and found it bitter, in connection with "that there
woman." After a pause, in which he sighed several
times, he remarked in his tired and gentle voice:

"There's two kinds of sadness, gentlemen. There is
the melancholy sadness that has been with you for so
long that you have got used to it and kind o' enjoy it in
a way. And then there's the kind o' sadness where you
go back on yourself, where you make your own mistakes and fall below your own standards, and that is
a mighty bitter kind of sadness."

He paused again, while the skin wreathed itself into
funeral wreaths about his face, and then he said, im-
pressively:

"Both of them kinds of sadness I have known. First
I knowed the melancholy kind, and now I know the bitter kind."

The first sadness that I had lasted for years (said
the stranger with the strange skin). It was of the
melancholy kind, tender and sort o' sweet, and if I had
been the right kind of a man I woulda stuck to it and
kept it. But I went back on it. I turned my face away
from it. And in going back on it I went back on all them
old, sad, sweet memories, like the song tells about, that
was my better self. And that is what caused the sad-

ness I am in the midst of now. It's the feelin' that I done wrong in turnin' away from all them memories that makes me as sad as you see me today. I will first tell you how the first sadness come onto me, and secondly, I will tell you how I got the sadness I am in the midst of now.

Gentlemen, mebby you have noticed that my skin is kind o' different from most people's skin. That is a gift, and there was a time when I made money off'n that gift. And I got another gift. I'm longer and slimmer than most persons is. And besides them two gifts, I got a third gift. I can eat glass, gentlemen, and it don't hurt me none. I can eat glass as natural and easy as a chicken eats gravel. And them three gifts is my art.

I was an artist in a side show for years, gentlemen, and connected with one of the biggest circuses in the world. I could have my choice of three jobs with any show I was with, and there ain't many could say that. I could be billed as the India Rubber Man, on account of my skin; or I could be billed as the Living Skeleton, on account of my framework; or I could be billed as the Glass Eater. And once or twice I was billed as all three.

But mostly I didn't bother much with eating glass or being a Living Skeleton. Mostly I stuck to being an India Rubber Man. It always seemed to me there was more art in that, more chance to show talent and genius. The gift that was given to me by Providence I developed and trained till I could do about as much with my skin as most people can with their fingers. It takes constant work and practice to develop a skin, even when Nature has been kind to you like she has to me.

For years I went along contented enough, seein' the country and being admired by young and old, and wondered at and praised for my gift and the way I had turned it into an art, and never thinkin' much of women nor matrimony nor nothing of that kind.

But when a man's downfall is put off, it is harder when it comes. When I fell in love I fell good and hard. I fell into love with a pair of Siamese twins. These here girls was tied together somewheres about the waistline with a ligament of some kind, and there wasn't no fake about it—they really was tied. On account of motives of delicacy I never asked 'em much about that there ligament. The first pair of twins like that who was ever on exhibition was from Siam, so after that they called all twins of that kind Siamese twins. But these girls wasn't from none of them outlandish parts; they was good American girls, born right over in Ohio, and their names was Jones. Hetty Jones and Netty Jones was their names.

Hetty, she was the right-hand twin, and Netty was the left-hand twin. And you never seen such lookers before in your life, double nor single. They was exactly alike, and they thought alike and they talked alike. Sometimes when I used to set and talk to 'em I felt sure they was just one woman. If I coulda looked at 'em through one of these here stereoscopes they woulda come together and been one woman. I never had any idea about 'em bein' two women.

Well, I courted 'em, and they was mighty nice to me, both of 'em. I used to give 'em candy and flowers and little presents, and I would set and admire 'em by the hour. I kept gettin' more and more into love with them. And I seen they was gettin' to like me, too.

So one day I outs with it.

"Will you marry me?" says I.

"Yes," says Hetty. And, "Yes," says Netty. Both in the same breath! And then each one looked at the other one, and they both looked at me, and they says, both together:

"Which one of us did you ask?"

"Why," says I, kind o' flustered, "there ain't but one of you, is they? I look on you as practically one woman."

"The idea!" says Netty.

"You orter be ashamed of yourself," says Hetty.

"You didn't think," says Netty, "that you could marry both of us, did you?"

Well, all I had really thought up to that time was that I was in love with 'em, and just as much in love with one as with the other, and I popped the question right out of my heart and sentiments without thinking much one way or the other. But now I seen there was going to be a difficulty.

"Well," I says, "if you want to consider yourself as two people, I suppose it would be marryin' both of you. But I always thought of you as two hearts that beat as one. And I don't see no reason why I shouldn't marry the two of you, if you want to hold out stubborn that you *are* two."

"For my part," says Hetty, "I think you are insulting."

"You must choose between us," says Netty.

"I would never," says Hetty, "consent to any Mormonous goings-on of that sort."

They still insisted they was two people till finally I kind o' got to see their side of the argyment. But how was I going to choose between them when no matter which one I chooses she was tied tight to the other one?

We agreed to talk it over with the Fat Lady in that show, who had a good deal of experience in concerns of the heart, and she had been married four or five times and was now a widder, having accidental killed her last husband by rolling over on him in her sleep. She says to me:

"How happy you could be with either, Skinny, were t'other dear charmer away!"

"This ain't no jokin' matter, Dolly," I tells her. "We come for serious advice."

"Skinny, you old fool," she says, "there's an easy way out of this difficulty. All you got to do is get a surgeon to cut that ligament and then take your choice."

"But I ain't really got any choice," I says, "for I loves 'em both and I loves 'em equal. And I don't believe in tamperin' with nature."

"It ain't legal for you to marry both of 'em," says the Fat Lady.

"It ain't moral for me to cut 'em asunder," I says.

I had a feelin' all along that if they was cut asunder trouble of some kind would follow. But both Hetty and Netty was strong for it. They refused to see me or have anything to do with me, they sent me word, till I give up what they called the insultin' idea of marryin' both of 'em. They set and quarreled with each other all the time, the Fat Lady told me, because they was jealous of each other. Bein' where they couldn't get away from each other even for a minute, that jealousy must have et into them something unusual. And finally I knuckled under. I let myself be overruled. I seen I would lose both of 'em unless I made a choice. So I sent 'em word by the Fat Lady that I would choose. But I knowed deep in my heart all the time that no good would come of it. You can't go against Scripter and prosper: and the Scripter says: "What God has joined together, let no man put asunder."

Well, we fixed it up this way: I was to pay for that there operation, having money saved up for to do it with, and then I was to make my choice by chance. The Fat Lady says to toss a penny or something.

But I always been a kind of a romantic feller, and I says to myself I will make that choice in some kind of a romantic way. So first I tried one of these ouija boards, but all I get is "Etty, Etty, Etty," over and over again, and whether the ouija left off an H or an N there's no way of telling. The Fat Lady, she says,

"Why don't you count 'em out, like kids do, to find out who is It?"

"How do you mean?" I asks her.

"Why," says she, "by saying, 'Eeny, meeny, miney, mo!' or else 'Monkey, monkey, bottle of beer, how many monkeys have we here?' or something like that."

But that ain't romantic enough to suit me, and I remember how you pluck a daisy and say, "She loves me! She loves me not!" And I think I will get an American Beauty rose and do it that way. Well, they had the operation, and it was a success. And about a week later I'm to go to the hospital and tell 'em which one has been elected to the holy bonds of matrimony. I gets me a rose, one of the most expensive that money can buy in the town we was in, and when I arrive at the hospital I start up the front steps pluckin' the leaves off and sayin' to myself, "Hetty she is! Netty she is! Hetty she is!"—and so on. But I never got that rose all plucked.

I knowed all along that it was wrong to put asunder what God had joined together, and I orter stuck to the hunch I had. You can't do anything to a freak without changing his or her disposition some way. You take a freak that was born that way and go to operating on him, and if he is good-natured he'll turn out a grouch, or if he was a grouch he'll turn out good-natured. I knowed a dog-faced boy one time who was the sunniest critter you ever seen. But his folks got hold of a lot of money and took him out of the business and had his features all slicked up and made over, and what he gained in looks he lost in temper and disposition. Any tinkering you do around artists of that class will change their sentiments every time.

I never got that rose all plucked. At the top of the steps I was met by Hetty and Netty, just comin' out of the hospital and not expectin' to see me. With one of them was a young doctor that worked in the hospital, and with the other was a patient that had just got well. They explained to me that as soon as they had that operation their sentiments towards me changed. Before, they had both loved me. Afterwards, neither one of 'em did. They was right sorry about it, they said, but they had married these here fellows that morning in the hospital, with a double wedding, and was now starting off on their wedding trips, and their husbands would pay back the operation money as soon as they had earned it and saved it up.

Well, I was so flabbergasted that my skin stiffened up on me, and it stayed stiff for the rest of that day. I never said a word, but I turned away from there a sad man with a broken heart in my bosom. And I quit bein' an artist. I didn't have the sperrit to be in a show any more.

And through all the years since then I been a saddened man. But as time went by there come a kind of sweetness into that sadness, too. It is better to have loved and lost than never to have loved at all, like the poet says. I was one of the saddest men in the world, but I sort o' enjoyed it, after a few years. And all them memories sort o' kept me a better man.

I orter stuck to that kind of sweet sadness. I orter knowed that if I went back on all them beautiful memories of them girls something bitter would come to me.

But I didn't, gentlemen. I went back on all that sentiment and that tenderness. I betrayed all them beautiful memories. Five days ago, I went and married. Yes, sir, I abandoned all that sweet recollection. And I been livin' in hell ever since. I been reproachin' myself day and night for not provin' true and trustworthy to all that romantic sadness I had all them years. It was a sweet sadness, and I wasn't faithful to it. And so long as I live now I will have this here bitter sadness.

The stranger got up and sighed and stretched himself. He took a fresh chew of tobacco and began to crank his flivver.

"Well," said Ben Grevis, "that is a sad story. But I don't know as you're sadder, at that, than the Widder Watson is."

The stranger spat colorfully into the road, and again the faint semblance of a smile, a bitter smile, wreathed itself about his mouth.

"Yes, I be!" he said. "I be a sadder person than the Widder Watson. It was her I married!"